LEGEND AND LL␣

SHADOW OF WHITE
BOOK 3

Blake J Soder

Copyright © 2017 Blake J Soder

All rights reserved

The characters and events portrayed in this book are fictitious. Any similarity to real persons, living or dead, is coincidental and not intended by the author.

No part of this book may be reproduced, or stored in a retrieval system, or transmitted in any form or by any means, electronic, mechanical, photocopying, recording, or otherwise, without express written permission of the publisher.

ONE

Mira stared doubtfully at the dead chipmunk in the snare. The little rodent was hardly worth the effort it would take to skin and clean it. She might get two, maybe three small bites of meat off it if she was lucky. But of the five snares she'd set last night, this was the only one that caught something, and she hadn't made it this far by being picky.

Releasing the wire from the rodent's neck, she put the snare in her coat pocket with the others and turned to head back to camp, carrying the chipmunk by its tail.

She stopped after a few steps at the sight of a large, gray wolf coming down the trail towards her. It was trotting with its head down and a large, dead rabbit swinging from its jaws. When it reached her, the wolf stopped and dropped the rabbit to the ground at her feet. It then sat back on its haunches and glanced off to its right, as if there was something far more interesting than Mira in the tall prairie grass west of the tree line.

"What's this?" she asked, picking the rabbit up by the back legs and holding it in the air. "A pity rabbit?" She fixed her gaze on the wolf. "What? You think I can't catch my own? Or are you just showing off again?"

The wolf flicked a brief glance to her and then went back to watching the prairie, licking the taste of the rabbit from its muzzle. Seska, as Mira had named her, was two years old and large for a gray wolf, with unusual amber eyes. Sitting on her haunches as she was, she was almost as tall as Mira and easily outweighed the girl by a good forty or fifty pounds.

"Okay, fine," she said with an exaggerated sigh. "I'll accept your charity but only because I don't want to hurt your feelings."

Seska turned her head back to Mira and wagged her tail.

Still holding the rabbit in one hand and the chipmunk in the other, Mira leaned forward and hugged the wolf around her neck. Seska's tale wagged faster, brushing the trail behind her clear of leaves and twigs.

At twelve years old, Mira had blue eyes and blonde hair that fell just past her shoulders. She was dressed in several layers of old clothes that were tattered and frayed but provided adequate protection against the chill of the summer morning. She had been on her own for most of a year now, surviving by hunting, trapping, fishing, and collecting fruits, nuts, berries, and wild vegetables where she could find them. She was skilled at survival, not relying on Seska to hunt for her but grateful for it just the same.

"Come on," she said, releasing the wolf from her hug. "Let's go cook these up for breakfast. And just to show you how gracious I can be, I'll let you have this *whole* chipmunk."

Seska led the way as they followed the narrow deer trail back along the edge of the woods to the small clearing where Mira had pitched camp the night before. Her tent was a faded brown canvas tarp folded in the middle, staked down at the corners, and held open at one end with a short wooden pole. It was small and easy to miss by anyone walking or riding past on the prairie but large enough to hold both Mira and Seska at night, allowing them to share body heat rather than depend on a campfire that could be seen at a distance.

They did need a fire for cooking though. So, while Seska disappeared back into the woods to continue hunting, Mira busied herself with starting the fire. After placing some thin wood shavings and small twigs on a bed of dry moss, she struck a spark into the tinder with a flint and steel. She was experienced in the technique, having done it nearly every day since she was seven years old, and it took her only two tries to strike a spark large enough to start the moss smoldering.

She blew gently on the moss until the first flame appeared. Adding more wood shavings, twigs, and then larger sticks, she soon had a small but reliable fire going.

Drawing her knife from its sheath on her belt, she gutted and skinned the rabbit and chipmunk before skewering the rabbit on a stick to roast over the fire. She set the rabbit guts and the skinned chipmunk aside for Seska as she'd promised. Mira knew the wolf brought her only part of its daily kill but she didn't begrudge her for it. She accepted what Seska brought her but she did not want to become dependent on the wolf for food. That could easily go very badly if she let her own skills lapse and then something unthinkable happened to her furry companion.

She cleaned her knife and slid it back into its sheath after a quick honing on her steel. It was a small knife, with a blade only about four inches long, but it was all she needed and she kept it razor sharp.

Digging into her knapsack, Mira found her small leather pouch filled with the wild raspberries, mulberries, and small, green apples she'd come across yesterday. She'd also found some wild strawberries, but those hadn't even been close to being ripe yet and they probably never would be.

Since the long winter almost twenty years ago, the old seasons as her father once explained them to her no longer existed. Mira had never seen either a spring or an autumn. Now, there were only two seasons – long, harsh winters and short, cool summers with an ever-fleeting transition between the two. Even now, in mid-summer, she could see northern-facing gullies and other places shaded from the sun still holding patches of snow. It was rare to find any sort of fruits, nuts, berries, or vegetables that were adapted to the new climate. What she did find was usually small and never quite ripe.

She took a few of the raspberries and all the mulberries from her pouch and set them aside to go with the rabbit. She set two of the green apples on a flat stone in the center of the campfire to roast and soften a bit.

Either brought back by the smell of cooking meat or just good timing, Seska returned as Mira was taking the rabbit off the fire. The wolf quickly cleaned up the pile of organs and then crunched and swallowed the chipmunk, bones and all.

Mira ate half the rabbit, along with the berries and one of the roasted apples. The other she gave to Seska as a treat. She sliced the rest of the rabbit meat into thin strips, rubbed a bit of salt from her meager supply onto each, and set them on the flat stone in the center of the fire to dry. When the jerky strips were done, she stored them away in another leather pouch where they would last for several days. She rolled up the tent, pole, and stakes and then tied them to the top of her canvas knapsack with her bedroll. Finally, she poured a little water over the remains of the fire, kicked dirt over it, and then stomped it down.

She scattered leaves and twigs over the whole campsite and then quickly checked for anything she'd missed. It was impossible to erase every trace of her presence, but unless someone was following her, anyone who stumbled across this place and recognized it as a campsite would have no idea of when she'd been here or which direction she'd gone. Satisfied with her efforts, Mira set off with Seska again, the wolf happily trotting along a few feet ahead of her.

As they'd been doing for the past few months, they traveled south just inside the tree line, roughly following an old highway about a quarter mile to the east. She never traveled on the highway or out in the open if she could help it, always remembering what her father told her before he died.

You're a young girl in a big world with no rules or laws. Travel quiet. Leave no trace. Be a ghost in the woods.

He also told her to avoid people, especially men. But in the months since she'd struck out on her own, she had yet to encounter even one other person. It sometimes made her wonder just how big this world was and if she was the only human still living in it.

The highway itself was mostly impassible anyway. According to her father, it had been forty years since the old world ended. Time and nature had not been kind to the works of man. Recognizable mostly by the difference in vegetation, the old highway was little more than crumbling chunks of broken pavement hidden beneath a thick growth of weeds, grass, brambles, and smaller trees. Those random chunks and the hidden cracks in the old highway could easily lead to a twisted ankle or broken leg.

By mid-day, they reached what remained of several houses and smaller buildings. It was the northern edge of an old city she had been seeing in the distance for the past two days. She usually avoided going directly through any of the old ruins. Like the highways, the crumbling cities were dangerous in their decay and held very little in the way of food or water. But this city was too big and spread out. To go around it would take at least two days. She would just have to be careful and get through it as fast as she could.

Mira had, in fact, been through a couple of smaller towns before, but they were abandoned long ago. Her father told her the cities were much the same. Survivors of the old world and later the long winter lived in them for a while. But eventually the weather turned colder, the food ran out, and people left the cities to migrate south. Still, her father warned, there were sometimes stragglers, people who stayed behind, scavenging for what little might still be found. After enough time, these people would have lost all pretense to humanity. They would be hungry, desperate, and likely dangerous.

Glancing to the sky, she considered if they still had enough time to skirt through the edge of the city and be out of it and back in the woods by evening. Though she was fascinated by things of the old world, she did not want to be in any of the old cities or towns at night. She was accustomed to the challenges and dangers of the woods and prairies, but she knew little about what might prowl these ancient ruins once the sun went down.

She glanced to Seska, who was sitting patiently on her haunches beside her.

"What do you think, girl? Should we do this now or wait until morning?"

Seska returned her glance and then turned back to the ruins ahead. She gave a single bark toward the city.

"Okay. But if we get maimed or killed, it's all on you."

Like the old roads and highways, nature was quickly reclaiming the city. The streets and sidewalks were visible only as occasional patches of broken concrete in the overgrowth of brush, vines, and trees. Most of the houses and smaller wooden buildings had collapsed and rotted away long ago, while other structures of stone, brick, or concrete still held their general shapes. Even so, these often looked ready to crumble in the next strong wind or heavy snow.

Despite the sometimes rough going and tricky footing, Mira kept to the center of the old street so she could keep a safe distance from the ruined buildings on either side. She didn't know if there was anyone in them or not – probably not – but she wasn't taking any chances. Seska's keen senses would undoubtably alert her to any hidden danger, but she wanted plenty of running room just in case this place wasn't as abandoned as it appeared.

She intended to keep to the edge of the city where the ruins were smaller and the overgrowth of trees gave her a more familiar and safer feeling. But after a couple of hours, they came upon a flooded area extending at least a mile ahead of them and even farther to the east. A river once running through the city was in the middle of a slow course change. Because of the flooding, they were forced to detour farther west and deeper into the ruins.

Soon, they were in the center of the city, where multi-story buildings towered over them all around. Mira had to crane her neck back and look straight up to see their full height. Creaking under their own weight, some of the buildings were leaning at precarious angles, threatening to come crashing down at any moment. Birds flew in and out of the cavernous openings high above where thick glass once barred their passage. The glass now lay on the sidewalks and streets. A few of the buildings had already collapsed and lay in huge piles of rubble.

Rusting hulks of cars and trucks, some crushed by falling debris, sat partially hidden in the thickets of weeds and brush all along the streets. Their metal shells provided ready-made homes for mice, rats, opossums, raccoons, and other small animals.

While Seska padded quietly alongside her, Mira's caution and nervousness at passing through the ruins slowly gave way to awe as she marveled at the buildings and machines of the old world. Even in their decayed state, they told the story of a once-vibrant civilization full of people and commotion and noise. Thousands of people once lived here, raised these buildings, walked these streets, drove these cars. They got married, raised families, lived, laughed, and made plans for the future. Her father told her there was once billions of people in cities like this all over the world.

She could only imagine such a crowded, busy world. She'd read and seen pictures about it in some of the old books her father used to bring her. She especially loved pictures of cities at night, with crowds of people walking brightly lit streets beneath towering buildings of glass and light. In her own life, she had known only the woods, a small house by the river, and less than a dozen people for a brief time.

The sound of bricks and concrete crashing to the ground behind her jarred Mira out of her thoughts. She turned to see a cloud of dust rising from where the top corner of a building across the street had just crumbled, battering and crushing the shell of a small car beneath it. About a dozen terrified fieldmice scampered out of the billowing dust and quickly found temporary shelter among the surrounding weeds and other debris.

The sudden collapse and the continuing decay of the city around her reminded her this whole place was little more than a graveyard now, and a dangerous one at that. The old world was done. It lay in the ruins all around her and existed now only in old stories handed down from one generation to the next, or in the few books remaining from that time. The new world, her and Seska's world, lay beyond these ruins in the vast forests and plains now reclaiming the land.

Glancing to the sky again, Mira saw it was already well past midday. Because of their constant direction changes to avoid flooded areas and collapsed buildings, this detour was taking longer than she'd hoped. There was no way they were going to get through this city and back into the woods by sunset. The best she could hope for was to reach the southern edge of the ruins. There, they would have to find someplace safe to stay for the night.

She quickened her pace, which was just fine with Seska, who could trot faster than Mira could jog. They made another detour around another collapsed building and came to a large, concrete structure with several open, flat levels. About two dozen cars and a few trucks were scattered among the small trees, bushes, and vines growing on each level.

It was a parking ramp. Mira had seen pictures of similar structures. When people drove their cars into the city, they often parked them in these ramps while they shopped or went to work in one of the buildings.

She was considering cutting through the first level rather than going around it when Seska suddenly went on the alert. The wolf lowered her head and her ears went back as she uttered a low growl and barred her teeth. The fur along her spine was standing up – going ridgeback, as Mira called it – and her gaze was focused on the structure in front of them.

"What is it, girl?" Mira whispered, placing one hand on the back of Seska's neck and the other on the hilt of the knife in her belt. She studied the structure and saw several small, dark shapes moving quickly between the old cars and clumps of brush on the lower level, darting from one hiding place to the next. They looked like skinny, naked apes, not much larger than Seska.

She felt a sudden tightness in her stomach. She knew what these animals were. She had never seen one before, but her father had warned her about them. Though few in number and usually found only in the larger cities, they were probably the most dangerous creatures one could encounter.

Ferals.

TWO

Mira's gaze moved to the upper levels of the parking ramp. There were two or three ferals on each level darting among the cars and overgrowth. While there were ramps connecting each level, the creatures ignored them and jumped or dropped from one floor to the next until they were all on the lowest level.

"Easy, girl," Mira urged as Seska uttered another low growl. She kept her hand on the back of the wolf's neck. "Don't pick a fight unless you intend to finish it. And I don't think we want to tangle with these things."

Ferals were the descendants of people born shortly after the end of the old world. Many of that first generation were deformed. Most did not survive long. But of those that did, many were orphaned, abandoned, or otherwise forgotten in the cities. If they were old enough to survive and lucky enough to find food and water, they mostly raised themselves. They lived on anything they could find – rats, birds, insects, even fungus and patches of moss – and often interbred, producing the small, apelike offspring now congregating at the bottom of the parking structure.

They were a small subspecies now, no longer entirely human. But they retained much of their intelligence and were clever, fast, and agile, perfectly adapted to living and hunting in these ruins. They were also ruthless, cannibalizing their own injured or dead and attacking larger animals in packs.

Mira began to take slow, careful steps backwards, urging Seska to follow her.

"Come on, girl. Let's go another way, nice and slow."

Though the ferals had obviously seen them, the creatures were staying in the bottom of the structure, watching but not approaching. That could change in a heartbeat if she turned and ran. Then she would become prey.

Seska retreated with her but stayed on the alert. Continuing down the center of the street, they both kept their eyes on the parking ramp, glancing away only briefly to keep from stumbling over clumps of brush or random debris in the road.

A few of the ferals left the ramp and kept pace with them for a little way, darting from one hiding place to another, but most stayed in the structure. Mira was sure it was Seska that was keeping them from attacking. As much as she didn't want Seska to tangle with the ferals, they were probably equally cautious about messing with a wolf, unsure if it was part of a larger pack or not.

As they continued moving down the street, the ferals stalking them dropped off one by one until Mira couldn't see any more following them. Still, Seska stayed on the alert for another quarter mile or so before resuming her normal gait. When she did, Mira finally allowed herself to breathe a sigh of relief. At last, she could give her full attention to getting out of these ruins as quickly as possible.

By late afternoon, they were through the main part of the city and its crumbling buildings. They passed through a burned-out section where only charred concrete and stone foundations remained. An hour or so after that, nearing evening, they finally reached the southern edge of the city. They were now in a residential area where many of the houses were still standing but slowly being swallowed up by the encroaching woods.

Rather than try to find a house that might not collapse on them before morning, Mira shrugged off her knapsack and set her tent up in a relatively clear patch under some trees in front of one of the old houses. She then went about collecting scraps of wood for a campfire while Seska trotted off for an evening hunt.

"Don't bring back any rats!" Mira called after the departing wolf. A few weeks ago, they passed by a small town to the north and Seska returned from her evening hunt with the biggest rat she had ever seen, larger than a squirrel. She cleaned and roasted the rodent but the meat was bitter and tough.

"From now on," she explained to the wolf, "rats are strictly desperation food. Only if we're starving, and maybe not even then."

From the house next to where she set up camp, she collected some old planks from a section of the collapsed porch. She paused for a moment, looking up at the house. She didn't often enter any of the old buildings. They were almost always dangerous, with weak floorboards that could suddenly disintegrate under even her weight. But with Seska out hunting and her campfire not yet lit, she found herself considering a little exploration. Besides, this house looked a little sturdier than most. It was made of brick and had a tile roof, both of which would have helped slow the rot and deterioration of the supporting wood.

Setting the pile of wood down, Mira cautiously climbed the steps to the porch, testing each before committing her full weight. The boards were soft and spongey but still strong enough to support her. Instead of trying the front door – she figured it probably wouldn't budge anyway – Mira pulled herself up and through what was left of a window overlooking the porch. Like most windows in these old buildings, its glass was lost long ago to wind and structural shifting.

Inside, the house was dark and dank, smelling of rot and animal musk. Generations of birds and rodents had called this house home over the years. The floor was covered with dirt, fungus, old leaves, and animal droppings. Skeletons of mice predominated, but here and there were the delicate bones of a few birds and bats along with the sturdier bones of a raccoon and a couple of cats.

Mira prowled the house, moving from room to room, examining the luxuries of old her father once tried explaining to her. The television set, which showed moving pictures combined with sound and sometimes music. People would sit on couches or chairs and stare at it for hours on end. Every house had one or two, sometimes more. Mira still didn't quite understand how it worked or why people would spend so much time staring at it when they could just as easily go outside and see people moving and talking for real.

On a shelf near the television was a radio, which played music but didn't show any pictures. Again, Mira didn't get it. Why have two things, one of which could do only half of what the other did? She didn't think her father really understood it, either. Like Mira, he was born into this new world and was only passing on what his own mother or father told him.

Making her way to the kitchen, Mira opened the cabinets and drawers, looking for anything that might be useful but was neither too bulky nor too heavy. In a drawer that fell apart as soon as she tugged on it, she found several candles and a spool of thread with a sewing needle that wasn't rusty. She put these into the pocket of her jacket. There was a small container of salt in one of the cupboards. The cardboard was peeling away and the salt was hardened into a solid block. She stripped the rest of the paper away and added the block of salt to her pocket. There were also a few rusting tin cans with bulging tops and bottoms but she ignored these. She had never come across any food from the old world that was even close to being safe to eat. The ferals supposedly ate the old food whenever they found it. If they did, their stomachs were much stronger than hers.

With evening coming on and the light quickly fading, Mira moved on to one of the bedrooms. The bed frame was still there but little remained of the mattress, only scraps of stuffing and fabric, shredded by generations of rodents collecting nesting material. Part of a human skull and two of the larger leg bones lay on the floor next to the old bed frame. The bones were almost completely gnawed away by rodents. Mira guessed they were probably the remains of one of the victims of whatever calamity befell the old world. She'd come across other bones before, mostly in bedrooms like this one and sometimes in the old vehicles along the overgrown roads.

She often wondered what disaster could possibly have been so large it killed almost everyone in the world so quickly, most as they slept. Her father told her it was a storm of some kind. She'd heard others debate whether it was a war with unimaginable weapons, a deadly plague, or even a giant rock from space. But none of those seemed quick enough or large enough to have brough about the end of the old world in a single night.

She'd eventually decided it didn't really matter. Whatever happened, there was no going back and fixing it. All anyone could do now, her father once said, was survive and keep moving forward.

On a dresser next to the bed was a wooden box full of jewelry. Mira picked through the various pieces, admiring the sparkle and brilliance of the colored stones in their gold or silver settings. She guessed some of the stones were diamonds and sapphires while others were probably emeralds, but she didn't know which were which. Her father told her people of the old world prized such stones, sometimes above all other possessions. It was just something else Mira didn't understand. Sure, they were pretty, but you couldn't start a fire with them, you couldn't use them for hunting, and you certainly couldn't eat them. They had zero survival value.

She dropped the pieces of jewelry back into the box and turned to a short bookcase along the wall.

Here were the only non-survival-related items Mira prized – books. Her father taught her to read at a young age and would bring her new books whenever he came across them. He would sit with her every night in their house by the river as she practiced reading aloud from his latest find.

Books, though, had fared poorly over the years, and it was becoming more and more difficult to find ones that didn't fall apart in her hands. As she ran her fingers along the spines of the books in the bookcase, the old covers separated and the pages crumbled into piles of yellowish-brown litter.

She was disappointed but not surprised. She tugged open a drawer beneath the shelf and caught her breath. There, sitting alone on the warped bottom of the drawer, apart from the crumbling books on the shelf above, was a thick, hard-cover book sealed in a clear plastic sleeve.

Holding her breath, wary of being disappointed again, she reached in and carefully lifted the book from the drawer. Someone – probably whoever's bones were scattered across the floor – had valued this book.

It felt solid. She opened the plastic sleeve and eased the book out. Carefully opening the cover, she turned some of the pages and marveled at the crispness of the paper and clarity of the ink. It was in perfect shape and, best of all, it was a story book complete with illustrations. The drawer and the plastic had kept it safe from rodents, bugs, and the elements all these years.

Closing the book, Mira slipped it back into its plastic sleeve and left the house, feeling as though she'd discovered a rare and valuable treasure.

As she dropped out of the window and onto the front porch, she turned and froze at the sight of half a dozen ferals surrounding her tent. They had dumped the contents of her knapsack onto the ground and were pawing through and fighting over her meager belongings.

They turned at the sound of her dropping onto the porch and began shifting away from each other, spreading out, using both their arms and legs to move. They snarled and grunted among themselves, sometimes barking, chirping, or making a high-pitched keening.

Having seen them only from a distance, their appearance unnerved Mira even more than the noises they were making. They had small bodies covered with reddish-brown fur and unusually long arms and legs. Their dark eyes seemed too large for their small, bulbous heads. And while they had large, elf-like ears, their noses were almost nonexistent – just two small slits above a wide, muzzle-like mouth filled with tiny, pointed teeth.

They didn't look human but they were descended from humans.

There was a large male, a smaller male, and four females. Remembering these things hunted in packs like dogs and wolves, Mira guessed the large male was probably the leader, the alpha.

She clutched the book to her chest, unconsciously protecting it, and cautiously stepped back to the window. The large male moved forward a bit, sniffing the air between them. The rest of the pack crept up behind him. Had they followed her and Seska from the old parking ramp? Or was this a different pack?

She dropped her right hand to the knife at her belt and slowly drew it out. She guessed any attack would come first from the alpha male. The rest would follow his lead. Remembering what her father told her about them cannibalizing their wounded, she hoped if she could kill the alpha or wound him badly enough, the others would attack him and give her a chance to escape back into the house. But as fast and agile as these things were supposed to be, that was a long shot at best.

"Go on! Get out of here," Mira shouted, hoping she was taking an aggressive stance. She held the knife in front of her, moving it slowly from side to side. She took a step forward.

The pack uttered a round of low, guttural growls. Two of the females made those high-pitched keening noises again, following them with rising yips that sounded like questions. The alpha moved forward again and the others followed. Mira locked eyes with him.

"Come on then," she said. "Let's get this over with." Bending at the knees but not breaking eye contact with the alpha, she placed the book at her feet and then rose back up, keeping her knife at the ready. She'd never been in a fight for her life but always knew it could happen.

If you're ever in a life or death situation, her father told her, *don't be afraid or worry about protecting yourself. You kill whatever is threatening you as quickly and violently as you can. Because that's what it's going to try and do to you.*

Feeling her heart hammering in her chest and her adrenaline surging, Mira focused on that single thought – she had to kill this thing quickly and violently.

The alpha hesitated, as if recognizing the danger this new prey represented. He glanced back to the others and then raised his head to sniff the air. The others also began sniffing, raising and turning their heads this way and that.

A loud, angry snarl came from the trees to the right and suddenly Seska was charging out of the shadows and right into the middle of the pack. Bearing one of the females to the ground, Seska clamped onto her neck with her jaws. With a violent toss of her head, the wolf broke the feral's neck and flung her to the side.

Instead of running like a pack of coyotes would, the other ferals, including the alpha, immediately turned on Seska, screaming and howling and swarming over the wolf, tearing at her with their teeth and claws.

If there had been four or five more in the pack, they might have stood a chance. But Seska was a large wolf, weighing nearly as much as the entire pack combined, and more ferocious in protecting Mira than anything the ferals had probably encountered before. Her thick fur protecting her from their sharp but small teeth, she grabbed one feral at a time in her strong jaws, either throwing it through the air with a toss of her head or holding it down with one of her large paws and tearing chunks of flesh from it.

One who had had enough tried to escape, but Seska leapt and landed on its back, bearing it to the ground. She clamped her jaws on the back of its neck and Mira heard the crunch of its spine.

Turning on the alpha male, Seska caught him by one of his long arms and ripped a large chunk of flesh away. Shrieking, the alpha also tried escaping but Seska brought him down and stood over him, clamping onto his neck and violently shaking her head back and forth.

As Seska continued shaking the alpha and tearing through his throat, the one remaining feral, the young male, ran for the nearby trees and disappeared into the growing darkness.

Seska growled as she shook the alpha a few more times before finally dropping his limp body to the ground. Standing over the dead feral, she looked around to confirm Mira was no longer in danger.

She let out a heavy exhale, realizing she'd been holding her breath the entire time. Seska trotted over to the porch and up the steps. She sat on her haunches at Mira's side and wagged her tail, as if the slaughter she'd just unleashed on the ferals hadn't happened at all.

Mira knelt and hugged the wolf tightly around her neck, paying no attention to the blood on her muzzle.

"Thank you," she whispered.

Seska licked her face.

She stood, wiped the bloody wolf drool from her cheek, and scratched Seska behind the ears.

"Took you long enough, though. I thought I was going to have to kill them all myself. Next time, show up a little sooner, will you?"

Seska huffed at her false bravado and then turned and trotted back to the corpses of the dead ferals, sniffing at each one before moving to the next.

"I think you got them all," Mira called to her, guessing the wolf was confirming the ferals were indeed dead. "Except the one that got away, of course. Maybe you're just getting slow in your old age."

Seska glanced to her and huffed indignantly. It made Mira wonder if sometimes the wolf really did understand what she was saying.

When Seska was done checking the corpses, Mira dragged the bodies to a small clearing in the trees well away from and downwind of her camp. She then covered them with as much dry brush and wood as she could find and set fire to the pile. She didn't want any curious scavengers coming by during the night or other ferals finding and cannibalizing the bodies.

Finally, she collected her scattered belongings and repacked what she had left into her knapsack. All of her food was gone but at least she still had her snares and fishing supplies. She would go hungry tonight, but it wouldn't take her long to catch more game.

She set her tent back up and started a small campfire next to it. Retrieving her book from the porch, she sat in the grass between the fire and her tent. Seska curled up next to her, resting her head in Mira's lap.

Mira took the book from its plastic sleeve and opened it to the title page. Before she'd learned to read on her own, her father would read stories to her every night. Later, when he'd become sick and too tired to continue their nightly ritual, she would read to him.

Those were some of her fondest memories. Her father had been her best friend and protector. Now it was time to continue the bedtime tradition with her new best friend and protector.

Holding the book in one hand while stroking the back of Seska's neck with the other, she began to read aloud.

"Alice's Adventures in Wonderland, by Lewis Carroll…"

THREE

Taking the small spool of fishing line from her knapsack, Mira tied a hook to one end and baited it with the kidneys of the squirrel she'd caught in one of her snares that morning. Tying the other end of the line to a short, heavy stick, she tossed the hook and bait into the river where the current slowed and the surface was nearly still. She then sat back against a tree to wait, letting the line run across her fingertips so she would feel even the slightest tug.

The old city and the ferals were three days behind them. Fortunately, they hadn't run across anymore of the small, dangerous creatures and she was glad to finally be putting some distance between themselves and the city. She decided if they came across the ruins of another old city, she would give it a wide berth, even if it meant going one or two days out of her way.

They were following the highway south again. Having come across a shallow, slow-moving river, Mira decided to take a break from red meat and try a little fishing for a change. She still set her snares along a likely game trail though, just in case the fishing didn't pan out. Seska had played in the river a bit, jumping and splashing about like an oversized puppy before shaking the water from her thick coat and trotting off deeper into the woods in search of game.

Gazing to the north across the wide, flat prairie on the other side of the river, Mira studied the dark blue line that stretched across the sky. She'd first spotted it yesterday morning. The line was still low on the horizon but it had grown a little since yesterday, so it was definitely moving south.

She guessed it was a bank of clouds caused by a slow moving weather front, but she had never seen anything quite like it. It was dark, dark blue, almost black, and it stretched in a knife's edge straight line all the way across from west to east, looking more like a solid wall slowly rising in the distance than the clouds of a weather front.

And the temperature had begun to drop too. It wasn't much, but it was noticeable. If the dark line on the horizon really was a weather front, it looked too far away and was moving too slowly to be causing the drop in temperature. But Mira had an ominous feeling the two were connected in some way. Something big was coming and it did not look good.

She remembered her father telling her about the long winter and how it lasted two and a half years. But he'd never mentioned how it looked or if anyone even saw it coming. Was she seeing the approach of another long winter? Or something else, something worse?

She felt a light tap on the fishing line, bringing her attention back to the river. She waited to see if it would repeat. A few seconds later, it did but it was still only a light tap. From experience, she knew it could be a small twig or other debris hung up on the line just below the surface, or a little bait-stealing fish nipping at the kidneys, or even a turtle. When the tapping didn't repeat a third time, she went back to gazing out over the prairie to the odd, dark line across the sky.

She'd dreamed of this two nights ago. In her dream, she was sitting along the bank of a river, staring out over a grassy plain to a wall of dark blue in the sky beyond. The blue wall was moving much faster in her dream, growing as it raced towards her until it filled the entire sky. She'd been scared and wanted to run but then realized there was no escaping it – it was too big – and so she'd stood and faced down the onrushing threat until she awoke with a start as a deep, freezing cold enveloped her.

It wasn't the first prophetic dream she'd had. She had dreamed of finding Seska as a puppy and of her father's death. She'd also had several smaller dreams over the years about mundane things that had come to pass. Though the dreams were sometimes a little too vague or symbolic for her to understand at first, they often repeated and their meaning became clear as she got closer to the time of the event they were predicting.

Her father had been fascinated by these dreams, discussing their possible meanings with her and encouraging her to explore them.

Staring at that dark line stretching across the northern horizon, Mira considered how it did look like a kind of dark blue wall. As it moved south and came closer, it would grow in size. The numbing cold she remembered upon waking from the dream may have been a warning about the drop in temperature she'd noticed the past couple of days. Something was definitely coming. But just what it was or how bad it would be hadn't been revealed to her yet.

A strong tug on the fishing line snapped her attention back to the river again. She jerked back on the line to set the hook and began playing the fish in, pulling back and then letting it go forward a little, quickly taking up the slack each time by wrapping the line around the stick. It took her the better part of ten minutes to finally pull the catfish out of the water and onto the riverbank. It was a big one. She guessed it weighed upwards of twenty pounds.

She dragged the fish back to her campsite and immediately began gutting and cleaning it. Seska hadn't returned from her afternoon hunt yet so she built the campfire up enough to allow for both smoking the fish and cooking whatever the wolf brought back, if she brought back anything at all.

As she sliced and salted the fillets, preparing them for smoking, she felt a dull rumble in the ground beneath her. Moments later, she heard the distant thunder of hooves and looked up to see three men on horseback galloping at full speed across the prairie.

She froze. Though she was well inside the tree line and across the river, all it would take for them to know she was here was for one of the men to glance to his left and spot her campfire. She didn't think the river was deep enough or flowing fast enough to prevent them from crossing if they decided to investigate.

In moments though, they were past her and angling more to the southwest, following the river. Mira let out a sigh of relief. She didn't know where they were going in such a hurry but at least it was away from her. She was glad she hadn't put any green wood on the fire yet for the smoke. The riders would surely have seen that.

As she went back to preparing the fillets, it occurred to her the three riders were the first living people she had seen since her father died almost a year ago, not counting the ferals, which she didn't consider as people. She wondered if they had come from the old city or if they were just passing through, traveling south like her. Either way, she trusted her intuition, and her intuition was telling her she was lucky they hadn't seen her. She would have to be extra cautious the next few days.

Her father warned her to avoid people, especially men. She was only twelve years old but she wasn't naive. She fully understood the dangers men posed to any woman or young girl they found traveling alone through these lands.

Seska returned from her hunt a little before sunset with a small, dead groundhog clamped firmly in her jaws.

"You're a little late," Mira said as the wolf deposited the groundhog in front of her. "We're going to have to wait until morning to cook that." She didn't want to take the chance the riders had stopped and set up camp somewhere on the other side of the prairie. They could still be close enough to see a fire in the dark.

She gave the wolf a good neck and back scratching as a reward and then skinned and gutted the groundhog, hanging it in a tree to wait until morning. She tossed the groundhog innards to Seska. The wolf snapped them out of the air, swallowing them in two quick bites.

"Yeah, don't bother chewing those," Mira chided. "I'm sure they taste better after they've been puked up at least once."

Seska licked her chops in agreement.

Though it was late in the day and she had already doused the campfire, it was still light enough to read. Mira took her book out of her knapsack and leaned back against a tree. Seska lay down next to her and got comfortable with her head in Mira's lap. By the light of the setting sun, she opened her book to the next chapter and began to read aloud. Though there was probably plenty of distance between her and the riders by now, she nonetheless found herself keeping her voice lower than usual.

FOUR

The snow was already deep enough to make walking difficult and it was still coming down – big, fluffy flakes with weight she could feel as they landed on her head and face. Above her, the sky was a deep, ominous shade of dark blue and the air was frigid, well below freezing.

She was plodding through a vast, flat prairie of tall grass, mostly buried now under the heavy snow with just the tips of a few blades still visible. In the distance, she could see a patch of trees, the leading edge of a stretch of woods, and a cluster of oddly shaped tents. Tipis, she thought they were called. She remembered reading about them in an old book. It was an Indian village.

As she approached the tipis, she could hear dull cracks and thuds coming from the woods as branches and limbs broke under the weight of the snow and fell to the ground.

She crossed a narrow, frozen creek and entered the small village. There were people here, standing in the snow but frozen as solid as the creek. To her left was a handsome man with long, reddish hair. He was dressed in deerskins, as was the woman just ahead of her and to her right. The woman was tall and slimly built, with black hair almost to her waist. A little beyond this woman was a shorter, heavier woman, also dressed in deerskins but wearing a dull green blanket over her shoulders. All three appeared to have been frozen in the midst of doing whatever it was they were doing when the cold hit. The oversize snowflakes were alighting on their heads and on the bluish skin of their hands and arms, but they weren't melting.

She walked past the silent, frozen people toward a larger tipi set a little apart from the rest. There was a large black bird painted just above the entrance. The bird had enormous, outstretched wings. She pulled the flap open and ducked inside.

The tipi was much more spacious than it appeared from outside. There was a small campfire surrounded by white stones burning in the center of the bare, dirt floor. An old woman, older than any person Mira had ever seen, was seated cross-legged on a drab, brown blanket on the other side of the fire. Her head was down and her hands were folded in her lap. She was also dressed in deerskins. A colorful red, green, and blue blanket lay across her shoulders.

Unlike the frozen people outside, the old woman's skin was not blue.

She knelt on the folded blanket on this side of the fire. She sat quietly, watching the old woman, listening to the crackle of the fire, feeling its warmth. She did not wonder why she was here or what she was waiting for. She felt this was where she was supposed to be.

After a couple of minutes, the old woman raised her head and opened her eyes.

Mira awoke with a start, sitting up quickly and gasping for breath. Disturbed by her movement, Seska lifted her own head and turned to look at her, making a low whine.

She placed her hand to her chest and felt her heart thudding. She realized she was close to hyperventilating and forced herself to take deep, slow breaths.

The dream was still fresh in her mind – the heavy snow, the frigid cold, and the frozen bodies in the Indian village. What startled her awake was not the old woman looking at her, but the feeling the old woman actually *saw* her. In the instant their eyes met, Mira was suddenly sure she and the old woman were really sitting there in that tipi, looking at each other, as if it wasn't a dream at all.

She sat for a while, feeling herself calming down while replaying the details of the dream in her mind. It felt as real to her as sitting beside Seska right now. She was sure it was another prophetic dream, and she was sure it was connected to the previous one about the blue wall of clouds. She had a suspicion now of what they meant – something her father told her a few months before he died – but she didn't want to think about that. Not now anyway.

She took one final deep breath, let it out slowly, and then crawled out of the tent. It had snowed during the night. A thin layer of white covered her campsite and the woods all around. The snow reminded her of the dream and she glanced to the north. She couldn't see the blue line through the trees but she knew it was still there, a little closer again this morning. She remembered the color of the sky in her dream. It was the same blue-black color of that line to the north.

Suddenly, she wanted to break camp and get started heading south again as soon as possible.

Something bad is coming. Something very bad.

She was tempted to pack up camp and start out immediately, leaving behind her snares and the frozen, skinned groundhog hanging in the tree. But that wouldn't be smart. She had to be dedicated in her journey south. That much was sure. And she still had to eat along the way. She still had to survive. She couldn't always rely on Seska to bring her food.

Mira used a stick to stir the embers of last night's campfire and added a handful of dry grass and small twigs to re-kindle the flames. She was glad she'd had the foresight to store some dry fuel in the corner of her tent last night. Once the fire was going again, she added some larger sticks and then started into the woods to find more.

She stopped just a few yards out from the campfire and stared at the ground. There, in the snow – footprints. They came from the north right up to the edge of her campsite. Whoever made them had stopped and turned to face her tent for a while, standing less than ten feet from where her and Seska were sleeping. From here, the footprints continued to the south, disappearing into the trees.

The prints were large and widely spaced, made by a tall man with a long stride.

The tread pattern in the prints was unusual, more like the pattern she saw on some of the tires of the old cars and trucks. That meant the man's boots were probably handmade, so he most likely wasn't a raider or scavenger.

Curiously, there was a round imprint about two inches in diameter off to the side of each track on the right side. She considered the marks could have been made by a walking stick, but that would have to be a pretty big stick.

She looked around, searching the trees for any sign of movement or of being watched. Could he have been one of the horse riders? That seemed unlikely. The riders were already south of her. And why would only one of them have come through her camp?

Seska finally roused herself and stepped outside the tent. She stretched, yawned, and then padded over to Mira, stopping to sniff at the tracks.

"Yeah," Mira scolded her. "What are those? Footprints? Someone strolling through our camp last night? Some watchdog you are."

But, in Seska's defense, she had to wonder... How could someone large enough to make these prints have moved so quietly as to not alert a wolf in full view and sleeping only a few feet away?

It seemed impossible.

"Well come on then," Mira said. "Let's go check those snares and then get out of here. This place is getting too crowded."

Her initial concern about the footprints and her nighttime visitor began to fade the more she thought about it. Sure, it was a mystery, but whoever made the prints had apparently not been very interested in them. He had stopped and watched her and Seska sleeping in the tent for a while, but then he continued on his way. Whoever the mystery person was, he was probably two or three miles away by now.

They followed the footprints in the snow for a dozen or so yards only because they were going in the same direction as the game trail. The prints though, soon angled off to the southeast and disappeared over a hill. Seska followed the footprints while Mira continued along the trail, checking and retrieving the snares she had set last night.

Despite the game trail appearing to be well-used, the catch was disappointing. Mira returned to her camp with only a single squirrel.

She skinned and cleaned the squirrel and then roasted it over the fire along with last night's groundhog. As always, she sliced some of the meat thinly, sprinkled it liberally from her new-found supply of salt, and dried it on a rock in the fire so it would last longer. When she was finished, she put the strips of jerky into her leather pouch and then the pouch into her knapsack.

She was about to douse the fire when Seska returned with another large rabbit in her jaws, depositing it at Mira's feet. The wolf sat back on her haunches and looked up at Mira, wagging her tail, proud of herself.

Mira stared at the dead animal, feeling a flutter in her stomach.

The rabbit was already skinned and gutted.

"Oh my god," she murmured. She glanced up and scanned the trees in the direction from which Seska had come, expecting to see the maker of the footprints lurching towards her, mad as hell over the stolen rabbit.

"I think," she said slowly, still watching the trees, "it's time to leave. Right now. We'll cook this one up later."

She quickly doused the fire, packed up her camp, and started at a brisk walk south along the tree line, hoping to put as much distance between herself and the former owner of the rabbit as quickly as she could.

Seska trotted along beside her, looking not the least bit guilty of anything.

FIVE

Mira pushed herself as hard as she could for most of the day, stopping only briefly for a quick lunch of groundhog jerky and some wild asparagus and hickory nuts. By evening, she guessed they had covered nearly three times the distance they normally did in a day.

It was late afternoon when they stopped on the side of a hill overlooking a deep river valley. About a quarter mile to the southwest, across a sloping plain of tall grass and occasional trees, sat a small town next to the river. It was mostly overgrown and in ruins, but a couple of the houses on the far side nearer the river looked like they could be inhabited.

The river itself was wide and fast-flowing with steep banks. She could see an old iron bridge spanning it a little farther to the south. They would have to use the bridge to cross the river, and they would have to go through the southern edge of the town to reach the bridge.

She sat down on the side of the hill and dug her whetstone out of her knapsack. As she sharpened her knife, she cast occasional glances to the town below, watching for signs someone might be living in it.

Seska prowled around the hill for a while before joining her in watching the town and river valley. Mira took the stolen rabbit from her knapsack and tossed it to the wolf.

"There! You stole it, you eat it. We're going to have to run a cold camp tonight anyway and it will spoil by tomorrow."

Seska took the rabbit and lay down with it between her front paws. If she felt any guilt at all about it being stolen, she didn't show any sign as she gnawed and crunched away.

Mira went back to sharpening her knife. She glanced out over the valley, back to her knife, and then quickly to the valley again. She could have sworn she'd seen the figure of a man moving inside the tree line on the other side of the valley. She watched, carefully studying the edge of the woods for a while, her gaze moving from tree to tree, but the figure was gone.

If he was even there at all, she told herself. It had looked like a tall man with a large build, the size of man who could have made those footprints in the snow last night. But now she wondered if maybe it hadn't been just a trick of light and shadow caused by the setting sun.

"I think I'm getting a little paranoid," she said, glancing to Seska. "And I'm pretty sure you have something to do with it."

Seska ignored her and continued devouring the rabbit with loud crunching noises.

As the gloom of twilight settled over the valley, Mira studied the town again for any sign of life.

And there it was. On the far southwestern edge of town, west of the bridge, the window of a single house flickered with the faint glow of firelight from within.

"I guess someone is home."

She scanned the rest of the town but didn't see any other lights. In the morning, she would easily be able to cross into the valley unseen and bypass the one occupied house to get to the bridge.

Instead of setting up her tent, Mira spread out her bedroll on the ground and lay back on it, staring up at the sky through the tree branches. Seska, finished with her purloined rabbit, padded over and lay down next to her.

She couldn't remember falling asleep or even closing her eyes, but suddenly it was morning. The sun was already well into the sky when she sat up, blinking in the bright sunlight and feeling cheated out of the memory of a good night's sleep. The hard pace she'd set for herself yesterday must have worn her out more than she'd realized.

Seska was still fast asleep next to her.

"Come on, girl," she said, scratching the wolf's neck. "Up and at 'em. It's morning and we've got a bridge to cross."

Seska got to her feet, yawned, and stretched. Her ears suddenly pricked up and she stood staring at the town below. She gave a single huff.

Mira glanced down into the valley, following Seska's stare, and saw smoke rising from the edge of town. It wasn't heavy but it was darker than it should have been for a fireplace or even a campfire. She wasn't sure what to make of it but decided it was high time to get moving.

Quickly gathering up her bedroll and knapsack, she set off down the hill with Seska, angling her path to keep as many trees between herself and the town as possible. She didn't go directly toward the town. Rather, she skirted to the east of it, making her way to the riverbank where the trees ran along it all the way into town.

Twenty minutes later, they were approaching the bridge from the riverbank along the south side when the rumble of horse hooves stopped them in their tracks. She crouched down behind a clump of bushes and put her arm around Seska, pulling the wolf close and holding her still.

The three riders she'd seen two days ago came racing out of town on their horses and across the bridge. The one in the lead looked tall and lean with a short, reddish-brown beard. He wore a battered cowboy hat and a long, brown coat that flapped behind him. Of the other two, one was short and heavily built with a dark beard while the third was a younger man with blonde hair and a beardless face.

She watched from behind the tall grass of the riverbank as they thundered across the old bridge and disappeared into the woods on the other side. She waited a minute or two before standing and pondering on what to do next. She glanced to the town and wondered again about the smoke.

She didn't want to cross the bridge yet. Best to give the riders time to get farther away.

Deciding she may as well investigate the smoke to kill a little time, she climbed the bank with Seska and headed into town.

The town itself was little more than a main street and a few side roads. If the streets had ever been paved, they were now hidden beneath forty years' worth of dirt, grass, bushes, and trees. All the buildings she could see were well on their way to being reclaimed by nature. Just as in the city, and the other couple of towns she'd been through, most of the wooden structures were rotted away while brick and concrete buildings still stood, albeit with growing piles of rubble around them as they fell to decay more slowly. Here and there, the rusted-out hulks of cars and trucks sat nearly hidden among tall grass and saplings.

Making her way to the west side of town, Mira finally found the source of the smoke. It was a large, single-story house surrounded by a wide lawn. The lawn was fenced off into sections to hold livestock, a garden, and a small orchard. One corner of the house was blackened by a fire recently set but now out. The smoke was coming from a corner of the roof that was still smoldering. This was the house she had seen last night with light coming from the windows.

It stood apart from the surrounding houses in that the people who lived here had kept it in good repair over the years while the surrounding houses followed the town into slow decay and ruin. Most of the windows were still intact. Those that weren't had been covered by boards or heavy plastic. Multiple repairs had been made to the roof and walls over the years to keep the wind, snow, and rain out.

The house and the way the yard had been repurposed for livestock and farming reminded her of the house by the river where she had lived with her father.

The gates to the livestock pens were all standing open. A cow, three goats, and several chickens were wandering about both inside and outside the pens and in the garden. Past the animals and closer to the house, Mira could see the bodies of two people lying in the tall grass.

She considered turning around without any further investigation. She could wait for ten or twenty minutes before crossing the bridge and continuing south, never looking back. But the door to the house was open and she couldn't help but wonder if there was someone inside who might be in trouble.

She bit her lip and continued staring at the open door of the house for almost a full minute, not wanting to know any more about what had happened here but also unable to put aside her thoughts that someone might need help in there. If she was inside the house, injured and maybe dying, and someone else was outside, wouldn't she want them to come in and help her?

Seska, also staring at the house, gave a small whine and then looked at her briefly before turning back to the house.

"Okay, girl. We'll go check it out."

Glancing around self-consciously, feeling as though she was being watched but not seeing anyone, Mira crossed the front yard to the bodies lying in the grass.

They were both men. One was lying on his face while the other was on his side. Mira turned one over on his back and then the other. Their eyes were open and staring without seeing.

The older man looked to be in his early forties. His throat had been cut so deep she could see two of the vertebrae of his neck. He had also been stabbed at least three times in his chest and twice in his stomach. His face had odd, bulbous growths on it and his left arm was withered. Mira guessed he was of the first generation born after the old world ended, one of those born with deformities.

The younger man, maybe only in his late twenties, had been neither stabbed nor slashed. The left side of his head was caved in by a heavy blow from something like a rock or club. Just above his left ear was a mess of shattered skull, blood, and ruined brain matter.

The grisly violence threatened to turn Mira's stomach and she had to look away. She'd only ever seen one dead body before and that had been her father. But he had died peacefully in his sleep.

She leaned her head back and looked up at the sky, breathing deep, letting it out, and breathing in again. She knew the three horse riders must be responsible for this, but she couldn't understand why. Why had they felt the need to kill these two men so violently? She closed her eyes and cleared her mind of the horrific images she had just seen. And then she thought of nothing at all except the warmth of the sun on her face.

The feel of Seska licking her hand brought her back to the here and now. She looked down at the wolf and smiled, running her fingers through the thick fur between Seska's ears.

"I'm okay. Just had to take a moment there."

She turned back to the house and hesitated only a couple of seconds before starting forward. No matter what she might find in the house, she felt she had to finish this. Seska stayed by her side the whole way.

Inside, the house was clean and mostly well-kept, except for the furniture that had recently been knocked around and overturned. Another body lay on the floor in the living room. It was another older man, mostly bald, who had been hacked to death with a hatchet or some other large blade. He was lying in a wide pool of thickening blood.

In the kitchen, everything from the cabinets and cupboards had been thrown out onto the floor and countertops. A brutally slaughtered goat lay on a table with its guts lying in a pool of blood on the floor. Seska sniffed at the goat organs and was making as if to take a bite when Mira hissed at her.

"Seska! No!"

The wolf glanced over to her as if wondering what the big deal was. Then, accepting Mira's admonishment, she turned, sniffed at the floor, and trotted out of the kitchen and into the hallway. Mira followed her to a bedroom. Seska stopped just outside the doorway and stood looking into the room. Mira came up beside her.

In the bedroom, a young woman with long, brown hair lay spread-eagled on her back on a large bed. She was naked and her throat had been cut. Lying on the floor at the foot of the bed was the body of a girl with lighter brown hair and not much older than Mira. She was also naked and had been killed in the same manner.

"Jesus," Mira breathed.

She suddenly felt as though she was going to throw up or faint, or both. She turned abruptly and quickly stumbled back down the hallway and out of the house. Leaning over the porch railing, her stomach cramped as she retched onto the lawn. She hadn't eaten anything since last night and all that came up was a thin, watery mix of whatever was left in her stomach. After a few minutes, she thought she had it under control. But then she looked up and saw the two men lying on the lawn. All of the strength went out of her and she dropped to her knees. Her stomach cramped again and she dry heaved three or four times.

She felt Seska's nose against the side of her neck. She opened her eyes and wiped her face with her hand. Seska whined and Mira put her arms around the wolf's neck, pressing her face against Seska's thick, warm fur. The wolf let Mira hold onto her for as long as she needed.

After a while Mira wiped her face again and got to her feet. She took a deep, slow breath and looked down at Seska again.

"Come on, girl," she said. "Let's do what we have to and then get the hell out of here."

SIX

It was almost midday by the time they returned to the overgrown road that ran south to the bridge. In the town behind them, heavy smoke rose into the sky from the inferno Mira had started. It had taken a long time, but she managed to drag the bodies from the yard and into the house before setting it on fire properly, turning the building into a funeral pyre. She wasn't worried about the riders seeing the smoke and coming back. If they saw it at all, they would likely think it was from the half-assed fire they had tried to start themselves.

Crossing the bridge, Mira glanced over the side to the rocks and rushing water below. If, for some reason, the riders did return and she got trapped on the bridge, she would jump and take her own life before suffering the same fate as the woman and girl in the bedroom.

The riders were easy enough to track through the woods after the bridge. They had taken the most open route southeast. Mira stopped a little after the bridge and took her father's old map out of the side pocket of her knapsack and removed it from the plastic bag it was in. It had been handled and creased so many times it was nearly falling apart. Carefully unfolding it, Mira located the town she had just left and traced southeast. As she'd guessed, the riders appeared to be heading for the next small town along the river. If she and Seska headed due south, they could bypass the town by several miles and reconnect with the old highway in a day or two.

As she was carefully refolding the map, Mira once again got the feeling that she was being watched. Sliding the map back into its plastic bag and the bag into her knapsack, she carefully glanced around. The old road wound lazily between low, heavily wooded hills on this side of the river. The trees were so thick here she couldn't see more than a few feet into the tree line. If anyone was standing in those trees watching her, she wouldn't be able to see them unless they moved.

It couldn't be any of the horse riders, Mira surmised. They seemed hell-bent on reaching the next town on the river before sundown. And considering what they'd done to the family back there, Mira seriously doubted they would be simply watching her if they knew she was here.

Glancing to Seska, she saw the wolf was staring at the woods off to her left. She wasn't on the alert though. If there was someone in the trees watching them, Seska didn't consider them a threat.

Mira studied the woods, wondering if it was the same man she thought she'd seen last night and the possible maker of the footprints in the snow. He could also be the owner of the rabbit Seska had stolen. Was he following her or did he just happen to be in the same area? Whoever he was, he was better at being a ghost in the woods than she was.

"Come on, girl," she said, shouldering her knapsack. "Whoever he is, he doesn't want to be seen. Might be best to leave him alone."

They continued south, leaving the old road and cutting across the hills through the heavy woods. Even without reorienting herself with the sun to confirm her direction, Mira maintained a nearly straight trek due south. She couldn't explain her unerring sense of direction. Even her father had been both impressed and baffled by it.

By evening, they came to a wide, shallow creek. Mira set up camp on a bend in the creek completely surrounded by trees. Seska trotted off to hunt again while Mira set her snares and then took out her fishing gear.

As she sat on the bank of the creek with her line in the water, Mira again pondered the dark blue line running across the northern horizon. It was still moving south at a snail's pace. Nevertheless, it was noticeably closer and higher again today. Having watched it for several days now and considering how the temperature continued to fall as the line drew closer, Mira was sure now she knew what it was and what it heralded.

Her father told her about the long winter and how it lasted for two and a half years. It was brutal, killing a lot of people and animals. When it was finally over, spring and autumn no longer existed. Now, her father told her, it would just be longer and harsher winters every year, followed by ever shorter and cooler summers. Eventually, summer would also cease to exist and winter would reign year-round.

There will probably be one final, great winter, her father said. *It will be bad, worse than the long winter. It will be the beginning of a new ice age and it will last thousands of years.*

Mira felt certain now that what she was looking at was the leading edge of what her father had called the final, great winter. Her dreams seemed to confirm it. It was coming right now, and all she could do was try to get as far south as possible before its arrival.

SEVEN

The sky was heavily overcast and a cold, light drizzle was falling the next morning. Feeling they no longer had the luxury of waiting out bad weather, Mira packed up her camp and set out with Seska after a cold breakfast of left-over smoked fish and squirrel jerky.

The drizzle continued all day, turning heavier toward late afternoon until finally becoming a steady, freezing rain that began to coat everything with ice.

Seska trudged alongside Mira with her head down, looking miserable. Mira felt twice as miserable as Seska looked. She had dug the old rain poncho out of her knapsack, but it was too old and full of rips and holes to provide much protection against the wet and cold. The freezing rain continued to trickle down the back of her neck, soaking through her layers of clothing. Even her boots felt squishy and full of rain.

Despite her misery, Mira pushed ahead for most of the day, not wanting to set her tent up in the rain. She was hoping to find a natural shelter large and dry enough to accommodate both her and Seska as well as a small campfire. But as the afternoon wore on towards evening, she was getting closer and closer to admitting defeat and accepting it was her fate to freeze, drown, or die of pneumonia by morning.

At last, they came upon the old highway again. As if the gods of pain and misery were finally taking pity on her, Mira was relieved to see a partially collapsed overpass a few hundred yards down the road. The way the overpass had collapsed formed a kind of cave, open on one end but completely blocked by concrete, rubble, and twisted iron bars on the other.

There was enough dry grass, old leaves, twigs, and sticks in the cave for Mira to start a small fire. Searching under the largest of the surrounding trees, the ones providing the most shelter from the rain, Mira found some semi-dry wood to build the fire up. She stripped out of her clothes and draped them over small, stick tipis around the fire to dry.

Seska shook the water and ice from her fur and then promptly trotted out into the freezing rain again, disappearing into the darkening woods to do a little hunting. Less than an hour later, she returned and dropped a goose at Mira's feet.

"Where in the world did you find this?" she asked, lifting the goose by the neck. She'd never cleaned or eaten a goose before but she guessed it wouldn't be much different than a chicken or a pheasant.

Rather than pulling the feathers out, Mira found it was faster and easier to just skin the bird and get all the feathers out of the way at once. She then cut it apart and roasted some of the individual pieces over the fire while Seska cleaned up the heart, lungs, liver, and other organs. Mira sliced, salted, and dried the rest of the meat into jerky for later.

It wasn't until she finally sat down to read another chapter to Seska that the exhaustion of trudging through the woods all day in freezing rain finally hit her. Even before she reached the end of the chapter, her eyes were closing and she was drifting off.

As the rain continued to coat the woods outside her little cave with a thick layer of ice, Mira set the book aside and cuddled up next to Seska. She thought she should probably put out the campfire as she always did so no passersby in the night would see it, but she was too exhausted. Besides, she felt she both needed and deserved the extra warmth tonight.

What were the chances anyone else was out in the freezing rain and near enough to even notice the fire anyway?

EIGHT

The dream started out the same as before. She was plodding through the frigid air and heavy snow under the dark, ominous clouds, making her way across the frozen plain to the small village of tipis along the edge of the woods.

This time, though, there were no frozen bodies. The village was completely deserted.

She made her way to the tipi with the enormous black bird and peered inside. There was no old woman and the fire was long cold. Standing back and looking around the village, she wondered what she should do next.

Movement at the edge of the village caught her eye and she turned to see a grizzly bear slowly lumbering away, past a small gray tent that stood apart from the tipis and following the tree line south. As she tracked the bear with her gaze, she saw the old woman. She was standing in the clearing, looking at Mira but pointing to the bear.

Mira awoke suddenly and sat up, fully alert. She could hear horses snorting and frozen grass being crunched underfoot outside the cave. She quickly glanced around. The campfire had burned down to ash and the morning sun was sparkling off the ice-covered world outside. Seska was nowhere to be seen.

Fine time to be on a morning hunt, Mira thought and scrambled to her feet. She grabbed her knife and quickly but quietly moved deeper into the cave, putting as much of the concrete rubble between herself and the entrance as possible. Holding her knife in one hand, she picked up a short piece of rusty iron bar with the other and took a deep breath. Her heart was racing. She had no path of escape and no time to plan. If those sounds were being made by who she feared they were, she may have to fight for her life.

Within minutes, a man stepped into view just outside the overpass. He was tall, with a short, reddish-brown beard that accented his lean, angular face. He was wearing the same battered cowboy hat and long, brown coat Mira remembered from when she'd seen him crossing the bridge the other day.

Behind the cowboy came the two other men – the shorter, fatter one with long, stringy dark hair and a short, patchy, dark beard, and the thin younger man with blonde hair and no beard. The fat man had a long-handled hatchet tucked under his belt while the cowboy and blonde man had no weapons Mira could see.

"Ah… cozy," the cowboy said, glancing around the inside of the cave and then back to the other two. "I told you I smelled a campfire." He sniffed the air. "And meat. Is that pheasant?" He paused and glanced to the remains of last night's meal. "No… goose." He turned and looked to the back of the cave, his eyes finding Mira. "Did we miss breakfast?"

The blonde man gave an odd kind of high-pitched giggle while the fat man simply grinned, showing a mouthful of badly stained and crooked teeth.

"Come on out of there," the cowboy called to her. "We're not going to hurt you."

Mira stayed where she was. She had no intention of coming out.

"What are you doing out here all alone?" the cowboy asked. He kept his voice calm and soothing, apparently hoping she would trust him. "Are you lost? We can take you someplace safe, give you a hot meal. We even have hot water if you want to take a bath and get cleaned up."

The fat man gave a soundless chuckle. Mira knew everything the cowboy had just said was a lie. She didn't need the chuckles of a dirty fat man to tell her that.

"Did you come by way of that town down by the river? Did you know those people?" The cowboy reached up under his hat and scratched his head. "Were you hiding maybe, in one of the other buildings?"

When she still didn't reply, the cowboy turned to the blonde man and nodded his head towards Mira.

As the blonde man stepped forward, he raised his hands in front of himself, palms out.

"It's alright," he said in a cajoling tone. "We're not going to hurt you. We just want to make sure you're safe."

Mira had been holding her knife in her left hand. She laid it down on the concrete block she was standing behind so the man could see it and then carefully took a single step to the side, out from behind the block. She stood at a slight angle to him, blocking his view of the iron bar she held against the back of her leg. Her heart was pounding but she stayed focused. She had only one chance of getting out of this alive. She hoped she knew what she was doing.

The man smiled and lowered his hands. "You're very pretty you know," he said, still inching forward. "Do you like horses? You can ride with me on mine if you want." Now very close, he began reaching for her while asking, "What's your name?"

Mira gave him her best shy, helpless little girl smile and took a hesitant step towards him.

The moron fell for it.

Just as his hands were about to close on her shoulders, she lashed out as fast and hard as she could with the iron bar, aiming high. The end of the bar caught him across the cheek, just below his left eye.

The man screamed in pain and surprise, his hands going to his face as he stumbled back and fell over the concrete rubble. He struggled to get to his feet, fell again, and then shot an angry, hate-filled glare to Mira. Blood was pouring from his face and a rough, triangular flap of skin hung loose below his eye, exposing the bloody white of his cheekbone.

Mira quickly retreated back into the rubble again. She grabbed her knife and prepared herself for round two. They would drop all pretense now and come at her with determination. But one was now injured and that bettered her odds.

"God damn it," the cowboy growled. He turned to the fat man and barked, "Get her out of there. Now!"

The fat man, no longer grinning, pulled his hatchet from his belt. He stepped forward, circling to Mira's right.

"And don't worry about roughing her up," the cowboy said, stepping to Mira's left, blocking any exit that way. "As long as she's still warm, we can use her." He looked at Mira, his eyes narrowing. "And warm is optional for this little bitch." He reached under his coat and drew out a rusty, beat-up old saber about three feet long with numerous nicks and gouges in the blade.

The blonde man finally struggled to his feet. Raising one hand to his face, he gingerly felt the full extent of his injury.

"Jesus Christ, you fucking little bitch." He picked up a small chunk of concrete with his other hand and hurled it at her. "You're going to pay for this. I'm going to have a *lot* of fun with you."

Mira easily ducked the missile and circled around the rubble, placing herself closer to the fat man. She stood a better chance taking them on one at a time rather than waiting for them to all attack at once. The fat man looked to be the slowest of the three. If she could injure him, there was a clear path out of the cave right behind him.

The fat man hunched over and came towards her slowly, raising his hatchet in one hand and holding his other arm out to his side. He seemed wary now that she'd injured his partner. Mira didn't think he would hit her with the weapon. They wanted her alive despite what the cowboy said. But he could certainly use the hatchet to block Mira's own attack while trying to grab her at the same time.

She put one foot back to steady herself and made sure the fat man's attention was on the iron bar in her hand. She took a tighter grip on the handle of her knife, preparing to feint with the bar and then slash at the man's groin with the blade.

"Watch her knife," the cowboy warned.

Dammit.

A shadow fell over the entrance to the cave. Mira took a step back before flicking a glance to the entrance. All three of the men turned to look.

Blocking the entrance was a tall, broad-shouldered figure in a long, heavy, fur coat. He was silhouetted by the sunlight outside so Mira couldn't see his face or much detail, but she could see he was standing in a wide stance and holding a thick wooden staff firmly planted in the ground at his feet.

Any hopes she had of escaping after slicing the fat man were immediately dashed. There was no way she would get past the hulking figure now blocking the entrance.

From the corner of her eye, she saw the cowboy take a step back. He had a look of confusion and fear on his face.

"Jesus," the cowboy whispered. "It can't be." He raised his voice at the new arrival. "No! No, goddammit. You should be dead."

"Who da hell its?" the fat man asked in barely discernable English.

The cowboy hesitated before replying with a mix of fear and awe.

"The bear."

Surprised, Mira glanced back to the big man in the entrance. She hadn't heard that name in at least seven years. When she was younger, before her father had begun bringing her storybooks to read, he would regale her with tales about the bear that had both thrilled and intrigued her. But her father could spin a good yarn and she had always wondered if such a man really existed.

The bear, if that's who he really was, cocked his head a little and lifted his staff, holding it at a slight angle across his chest. His easy stance told Mira he was not afraid, even outnumbered three to one.

Seska stepped out from behind the man and stood at his side, head lowered, ears back, fangs bared. She uttered a menacing growl and went ridgeback again.

What the hell? Mira thought, seeing her faithful companion teaming up with a complete stranger.

"Oh Jesus," the blonde man said. "Jesus. That's... that's a fucking wolf!"

Seska launched forward, leaping and snarling, hitting the fat man full in the chest and knocking him to the ground. She immediately went for his throat. The fat man screamed and flailed at Seska with his hands, his hatchet dropped and completely forgotten.

The moment Seska attacked, the big man took two quick, long strides forward, bringing himself within four feet of the cowboy. In the shifting light of the cave, she caught the briefest glimpse of his eyes. They were hazel in color, but in them was a look she hoped she would never see again. It was the cold, uncaring look of death.

The cowboy raised his sword and backed away, stumbling over the rubble. "No," he pleaded. "You don't understand. We weren't going to hurt her."

In a simple, swift movement, the man jabbed the end of his staff forward, thumping the cowboy square in the throat before he had a chance to parry the attack with his saber. His weapon fell to the ground as his hands went to his throat. He stumbled back, eyes bulging. He tripped and landed on his butt. He tried to take two or three breaths but could only manage a high-pitched wheeze. Finally, his eyes rolled back in his head and he collapsed backwards into the rubble.

After jabbing the cowboy in the throat, the big man didn't wait for the results. He turned immediately to the blonde man and swung his staff from his side. The blonde man's hands went up to block the swing and Mira heard the horrible cracking sound of both his forearms being shattered. The big man quickly reversed his swing and brought his staff up and over the man's head, bringing it down horrifyingly fast and hard. There was a crunching sound, a spray of blood, and the blonde man collapsed to the ground like a pile of dirty clothes.

Seska was still straddling the fat man, her jaws locked on his throat. She was violently whipping her head back and forth while snarling like she had with the alpha feral. When the fat man ceased moving, Seska let go and stood over him, waiting to see if he would move again. His throat was a mass of raw, red meat and blood. His left foot twitched a couple of times but Mira was pretty sure he would never flash his filthy grin at anyone ever again.

She glanced over at the big man, finally getting a better look at him. He had long, brownish hair and a thick, unruly beard, both shot with gray. He was the biggest, oldest man Mira had ever seen, easily in his mid to late fifties, maybe even sixty. He had deep, weathered creases across his forehead and at the corners of his eyes. The bear-hide coat he wore, his age, and his appearance were more or less in line with how she'd pictured the bear when she was younger. And the deadly efficiency with which he used that heavy staff matched several of her father's stories.

Mira was convinced. This man was the legendary bear. He was real. But what was he doing here?

The bear glanced around at the bodies of the riders, confirming all three were indeed dead. It had taken him and Seska less than a minute to kill all three. When he finally glanced to Mira, his face was set in the same grim, hard expression as when he'd entered the cave.

Seska jumped off the fat man's corpse and darted towards him.

"Seska, no!" Mira cried.

NINE

Mira wasn't concerned for the big man's life. Rather, she was afraid the bear would hurt or even kill Seska. She had little doubt that killing a wolf would be any more trouble for him than the cold, efficient way in which he'd just killed two men. And hadn't he once killed a grizzly bear with nothing more than a knife?

Rather than lifting his staff to strike the wolf, the bear surprised Mira by lowering himself to one knee and then holding out his hand to Seska. She watched, dumbfounded, as Seska approached him, licked his hand, and then rubbed against him like a big cat. The bear's expression softened a little as he patted her on the side and then scratched her neck and back as if the two were old friends. He gave Seska a final pat and then got to his feet. Seska trotted back to Mira.

The bear stood with both hands on his staff, looking at Mira with his head slightly cocked. His eyes and face were back to their staid, grim expression.

Mira realized she was still standing among the concrete rubble with the iron rod in one hand and her knife in the other. She eyed the bear warily, not sure what to make of him or what the deal between him and Seska was. Seska had never been friendly with anyone but her. Even as a puppy, she showed affection only for Mira. She would let Mira's father pet her now and again but nothing else. She would shy away or growl if anyone else even got close to her. But she had stood at the bear's side, had helped him kill the riders, and now acted as if she had known him for as long as she'd known Mira.

She felt as though she was missing something.

The bear stood there for several moments, studying her. Then he abruptly turned and started back toward the entrance of the cave.

"Wait," Mira called.

He stopped, seemed to think about it a moment, and then turned back to her.

Mira laid the iron bar down, re-sheathed her knife, and stepped out of the rubble pile. She took a couple of steps toward the man and looked up at him. He was big, intimidating, and more than a little scary looking, but Seska had vouched for him and she couldn't ask for a better character reference than that.

"I saw you the other day," Mira said. "You were at the edge of the woods by that town in the valley. And you walked through my camp a couple of days ago, didn't you?" She was guessing at the first but she was pretty sure the prints in the snow outside her tent had been made by this man's boots and the heavy staff he carried.

After a couple of moments, the man gave a single, slow nod.

"You're the bear, aren't you? Like that man in the cowboy hat said. My father told me about you."

He made a low, non-committal grunt that was almost a growl.

"Are you following me?" Mira asked.

Now he gave just the barest shake of his head.

Mira frowned. "Can't you talk?"

The bear stared at her for another moment before replying in a low, gravelly voice.

"I wasn't following you. I was just... curious."

Mira had never thought about it before but she had to admit that a young girl traveling through the woods with a wolf at her side probably was a curious sight.

"Did you know them?" She glanced around at the dead riders, noting the soles of the cowboy's boots had giant holes worn clear through them. "That one in the hat and boots. He recognized you."

"A long time ago," the bear said. "I should have killed him then." He paused for a moment and then added, "I warned him I would kill him if I ever saw him again."

"They slaughtered a whole family. In that little town by the river."

He nodded but said nothing. She realized if he had been in the valley outside the town, he must also have seen what they had done. He was the one she'd felt watching her at the house and then after the bridge.

"Have you been following *them*?"

He nodded again. He certainly wasn't the chatty type.

"Well, thank you for stepping in when you did. I'm Mira, by the way, and this is Seska. But I have a feeling you two have already met." She remembered the cleaned and skinned rabbit Seska had brought to her. It must have been his.

The bear glanced at Seska and then back to her.

"What are you doing out here alone?" he asked.

His question caught Mira off guard. His tone was admonishing, like he had caught her doing something wrong. It made her feel she had to defend herself.

"I'm... I'm not alone. I have Seska." She reached down and stroked the wolf behind her ears.

"You are alone," he insisted in the same disapproving tone. "They were going to take turns raping you and then they were going to kill you, just like that family back there."

His blunt words made Mira cringe inside.

The bear continued staring down at her, as if contemplating her punishment.

"I know it's dangerous," Mira finally said, "but my father died last year. My mother died in the long winter. I don't have anyone else. It's just me and Seska."

He continued to stare at her but his expression had changed subtly, as if he was now wrestling between conflicting thoughts. Then, without another word, he abruptly turned again and walked out of the cave.

Seska trotted after him for a few steps and then stopped and looked back to Mira, as if wondering why she wasn't coming too.

She quickly picked up the extra layers of clothes she had laid out to dry last night and put them on. She then packed her knapsack, slung it over her shoulder, and hurried out of the cave.

The sky was mostly clear and the morning sun was just beginning to melt the ice from last night. She found the bear a few yards into the woods. He was stripping the bridles and saddles from the riders' horses and tossing them to the ground. When he was done, he slapped one of the horses on the flank and sent all three running into the woods.

"Why did you do that?" she asked. "We could have ridden them."

The bear bent down and picked up his staff before glancing to her again.

"Can you ride a horse?"

She had never ridden a horse before and realized she would have no idea how.

Taking her silence for an answer, the bear turned and began walking away again. His long strides carried him quickly in a southwesterly direction through the woods and away from the highway.

Mira followed. She had to practically jog to keep up with his pace. She was getting annoyed with this man and his disapproving looks and tone. Regardless of the stories she'd heard of him, who was he to judge her?

"We've been doing just fine on our own, you know," Mira said, "just me and Seska. Even if you hadn't come by when you did, I'll bet we could have gotten out of there. We might have even killed one or two of them on our own. Maybe all three."

"Who's 'we?'" the bear asked, not even turning around. "Your wolf wasn't with you." He continued walking as if he was trying to get away from her.

"You said you met that cowboy before and you let him live." Mira was almost out of breath from trying to keep up with him. "If you'd killed him when you had the chance, that family might still be alive. How many other people have died because you let one man live?"

The bear stopped and turned so suddenly Mira almost ran into him. The look in his eyes scared the hell out of her and she was suddenly wishing she could take back what she'd said. She took a small step back but then caught herself and defiantly held her ground, meeting his gaze though trembling inside.

Seska stopped and looked back and forth between them. She gave a small whine, sensing the sudden tension.

Thunder rumbled to the north. The bear broke his gaze with her and looked at the sky. The anger disappeared from his eyes. He turned and began walking southwest again.

Mira realized she'd been holding her breath. She let it out with a deep sigh before starting out after the man once more. His pace had slowed a bit but she still struggled to keep up. Seska trotted alongside her.

A few minutes later, thunder rumbled again and it began to rain.

TEN

The thunderstorm was threatening to drown everything in the woods with its constant, torrential downpour.

Cold and wet, Mira continued trudging after the bear with her head down against the rain. His pace had slowed but he never paused, stopped, or even looked back. Using his staff as a walking stick, he kept moving forward. The cold and rain seemed no more of a concern to him than the wolf and twelve-year-old girl dogging his heals.

More than once, Mira wondered why she was even following this man. He didn't seem as heroic or handsome as he had in her father's stories. In fact, he was kind of rude and brutish. It was obvious he didn't want her following him. He'd tried to outpace her, lose her, at the start, and he hadn't spoken a word or even looked at her since morning.

Was she just determined to be a pest because he had all but questioned her ability to take care of herself? Or was she following him simply because he was the first person she'd encountered since her father died who hadn't tried to kill her, had even saved her? Either way, the symbolism of her dream last night was not lost on her – the old woman pointing to the lumbering grizzly bear, and then a man known as the bear suddenly showing up. Had the old woman been telling her to follow him, or had she been warning her about the man. Mira didn't know and, frankly, she was too cold and wet to care right now.

A dark shape loomed out of the rain ahead. It was a cabin, built of mortared stone with a slate tile roof. As the man approached the front steps, Mira wondered if he had just happened across it or if he'd known it was here all along. She was inclined to believe the latter. It seemed too coincidental they would accidentally happen upon a sturdy little cabin like this in the middle of a thunderstorm.

The bear climbed the steps and shouldered the front door open. He stepped inside, leaving the door ajar behind him.

Mira followed up the steps and cautiously stepped in through the door. Seska pushed past her and showered the place with rain from her thick coat.

The cabin was relatively neat, clean, and orderly, considering most of the houses she'd seen. It consisted of one main room, a combination kitchen and dining area, two bedrooms, and a small bathroom. The windows were still intact and there were no holes in the roof that Mira could see. There was a small couch, a table and chairs, and a few other pieces of furniture that looked old but perfectly usable.

The air was cool and stale but lacked the usual aromas of mold, decay, and animal droppings.

The bear knelt in front of a large, stone fireplace built into the far wall. Split logs were stacked neatly to the side. He had taken his heavy coat off and laid it over the back of a chair. His staff leaned against the wall just inside the door. Beneath his coat, he wore deer skin pants, a tunic also made of deer skin, and heavy leather boots. She was surprised he didn't wear more layers, but then considered he probably spent most of his life outdoors and had grown accustomed to the cold long ago.

Mira pushed the heavy door closed and sat on the arm of the couch while the bear struck a spark into some kindling with a piece of flint and steel. The fire caught right away. He added some smaller sticks and then a few of the split logs. It occurred to her that she still didn't even know his real name. She remembered asking her father one time. He'd smiled and shook his head. "The bear is the bear," he'd said. "No other name suits him."

With the fire going now, the man sat back on a chair in front of it and leaned forward, his elbows on his knees and his big hands clasped in front of him. He stared into the fire, seeming to be in deep contemplation. He still had not acknowledged Mira's presence in the room. She didn't think he was intentionally being rude – he had left the door open for her after all – but he was definitely being inhospitable. Maybe he just wasn't used to being around other people.

She shrugged out of some of her rain-soaked layers and laid them over the back of the couch to dry. She moved closer to the fire and sat down on the floor across from the big man's chair. Seska padded over and lay down on the floor between them.

"I'm sorry," Mira said, "for what I said this morning. I don't have any right to judge you for what you did or didn't do in the past. You couldn't have known what that man would become, what he would do."

He continued staring into the fire. She was about to accept the fact that he was going to keep ignoring her when he finally spoke.

"I did know," he said in his gravelly voice while still staring into the fire. "But I let him live anyway, just to deliver a message. It didn't make any difference in the end."

In the flickering firelight, Mira noticed the scar on his neck for the first time. It was wide, running clear across his neck almost from ear to ear. She remembered the story of how the bear had been nearly killed while fighting another man for the future of some village. The man had been armed with an ax while the bear used only his staff and a knife. The bear was cut across the throat but still prevailed. If nothing else, it seemed proof this man was indeed the bear from her father's stories. And it had to be the reason his voice was so rough and grating.

Though sometimes he talked as though he'd known the bear for a time, her father never told her where the man came from. Maybe he didn't know, but Mira thought the bear's apparent age made it obvious.

"You're from the old world, aren't you?"

His eyes shifted to look at her and his brow furrowed a bit, as if he had never heard that term before.

"You know, from back when the cities were full of people and all the machines still worked," she explained. "My father told me about it, though he never saw it himself."

The man's frown disappeared. After a moment, he nodded.

"Do you know what happened?" Mira asked. "I've heard different stories, like there was a war, or some disease that killed everyone. My father thought it was some kind of storm but I think that's just another story. I've never met anyone who knew for sure what really happened."

The bear looked back into the fire. Mira held her silence. This was a man who put some thought into his replies before speaking.

After almost a full minute, the bear spoke again.

"It was a storm," he said, still staring into the fire. "It happened early in the morning. It was a Sunday." He paused and then continued. "When the sun finally came up, everyone was dead – people, trees, animals... even the sky." His eyes shifted to her again. "There were a few survivors, like me, but many of them died later."

Mira stared at him, realizing he had actually *seen* this storm, had been there as it happened and lived through it. That was something her father never told her. He might not have known. But now Mira knew and she wondered if she was the only living person other than the bear who knew the truth of it.

"What happened?" she asked. "What did it look like?"

Another long pause and then, "A bright flash of light, like the sun suddenly rising in the west, but it was green and brighter than the sun, brighter than anything I'd ever seen. The ground rumbled. It only lasted for a few seconds. And then there was a hot wind with lightning and ribbons of colored lights in the sky." He paused again for a moment and then shrugged. "Someone told me once it came from space, some kind of random cosmic event, but I don't think anyone ever knew for sure what it really was."

Mira pictured it in her mind – a storm of light and wind.

"And it killed everyone right away?"

He nodded but then added, "Some died later. They died the same way, just slower. Some kind of radiation, I guess. Some died at the hands of others and some by accident."

"How old were you?"

"Fifteen."

Oh my god, she thought, imagining herself in his place. He'd been only three years older than she was now. She thought of having lost her own father and never having known her mother. This man must have lost more friends and family in a single night than she had ever known. And where she had been born into this world, he'd had to adjust, adapt, learn to survive today or perish tomorrow. She didn't know if she could have made such a sudden and drastic transition from one world to the next, from one life to another.

They sat in quiet for a while, both staring into the fire. Between them, Seska closed her eyes and snoozed.

Finally, Mira glanced up at him and decided to try introductions again. "My name's Mira. My mother wanted to name me Miracle but my father thought it sounded goofy." She shrugged. "I guess they finally compromised."

After a moment, the bear asked, "Why Miracle?"

"Because I was born during the long winter. My father said a lot of people died in that winter but I was the only one born. My own mother died a few months later. And no one thought I would survive for long, but I did."

The bear nodded thoughtfully. She thought he was going to lapse into silence again but then he finally looked at her, his eyes a little less hard and his face not so grim.

"Erik."

ELEVEN

As Mira guessed, Erik did not just happen upon this cabin. It was one of several convenient shelters in the area he knew of – other cabins like this or old houses hidden in the woods.

"But you don't live in any of them? You don't have a home?"

Erik shook his head.

"I don't have one either. I used to live with my father in a house a long ways north of here. But he died and I couldn't stay there."

Stroking Seska's side as she snoozed by the fire, Mira asked, "So how is it you two know each other? I'm guessing that was your rabbit she brought back to my camp the other day. And she's never taken to strangers before."

"I gave her the rabbit," Erik said. "I had plenty. She's been visiting me for a few days now. That's how I came across you. She led me to your camp after you left the city back there."

Mira was surprised. "You were in the city?"

He nodded. "I came through just after you. I ran across where you burned those creatures."

"The ferals."

He shrugged. "Whatever you want to call them. I could see it must have been quite a fight. I saw the tracks of a large wolf and a small girl. It got me a little curious. Those three men had gone through the city ahead of you and you were going in the same direction. I wasn't sure if you were following them or if you didn't know they were ahead of you."

"I didn't know anything about them until they rode past my camp. It was the same night you must have walked through. I saw your footprints in the snow."

"I left those on purpose. I was hoping to make you think someone was following you so you would turn and go in another direction. That's why I gave your wolf the rabbit – so you could leave earlier and not have to hunt that day."

"But then we never would have met."

"You also wouldn't have nearly been murdered in that cave."

He had a point. But remembering her dream of the old woman pointing to the bear before she'd even met him, she was pretty sure their paths were destined to cross, one way or another.

Erik produced some venison jerky and dried apricots from the pockets of his coat while Mira brought out her strips of smoked goose and some black walnuts she'd found.

They shared their food and ate and talked some more as the thunderstorm continued to pound the woods outside. Mira asked questions about the old world and Erik confirmed or corrected her information with three or four-word replies. It was like talking to a living history book, albeit an abbreviated one. She wished she had paper and pencil so she could write down everything she was learning from him. But whenever she asked him about his own life, he gave only general answers or changed the subject completely. He didn't seem to like talking about himself.

"So, you've been living in the woods all these years, roaming about from here to there?" Mira asked. "Have you ever come across a town or village you could live in? You know, with other people."

"I've come across a few. Most are abandoned now."

"I'll bet they went south. You should head south too. That's where we're going, me and Seska. I think there's another bad winter coming, even worse than the long winter… a lot worse."

Erik glanced at the snoozing wolf in front of the fire.

"She hunts for you?"

"Sometimes," she said, wondering why he had suddenly changed the subject again. "I didn't train her or anything. She just does it on her own. My dad taught me how to set snares when I was little. One day, I found her caught in one of my snares. She was just a puppy and she looked half-starved. I think she was orphaned. My dad let me keep and raise her."

She paused, scratching Seska behind the ears.

"I think he knew he was dying even then. He seemed tired a lot of the time and he was losing weight. He tried not to show the pain but I could see it on his face sometimes. I think he figured that, after he was gone, a wolf would be a good companion and protector for me."

"Sounds like a good man," Erik said, nodding. "He did what he could for you. Don't ever let go of that."

She got up and went to her knapsack, retrieving the map from the side pocket. She brought it back and carefully spread it out on the table.

"This is where we're going," she said, pointing to a small spot near the bottom of the map. "Nova Springs. My dad said a lot of people headed south in small groups before the long winter. They were going to meet up there."

He glanced at the map but made no comment.

"Have you ever been south? My dad said some of the groups like the one he was in got stranded by the long winter but that some of them probably survived and made it all the way. Have you ever come across any of them?"

He glanced back to the fire and stared into it. "No."

She didn't believe him. He seemed uncomfortable with the subject and was keeping something to himself. She decided to let it go for now and refolded her map.

"Which direction are you heading tomorrow?" She asked as she stowed her map back into her knapsack.

He didn't answer. He continued staring into the fire, lost in thought.

Mira came over and sat down again by the fire next to Seska. She stroked the wolf's fur and looked back up at Erik.

"Are you going to stay here?"

He finally shifted his gaze to her. "Southwest."

"That's still south. Maybe we can travel together for a while. Keep each other company for a few days."

He hesitated a moment, gave a slight nod, and then turned his gaze back to the fire.

She felt a sense of anticipation she hadn't felt in a long time. Finally, she would have someone other than Seska to travel with, to talk to. And not just anyone, but someone from the old world who had spent most of his life surviving in the wilderness. Erik was someone who could teach her more about survival in a week than her father was able to teach her or that she'd learned on her own over the past year.

And she just knew that once they got going and got to know each other better, Erik would stay with her all the way to Nova Springs.

TWELVE

Mira was exhausted.

They had been walking steady for more than two days, resting only at night and starting out again at sunrise the next day. She pointed out the dark line of clouds to the north and told Erik her father's theory of a coming great winter. While Erik neither agreed nor disagreed with what the dark line represented, she wondered if it wasn't the reason he seemed to be pushing their pace so hard.

By midafternoon of the third day, the woods gave way to a great, wide prairie of tall grass and low rolling hills. Erik's long legs carried him easily through the grass while Seska enjoyed the challenge of bounding through it. She walked behind Erik in the trail he was breaking ahead of her but she still felt as though she was slogging through ankle-deep mud or wet sand.

On the bright side of things, the weather had remained clear since the thunderstorm and they were now traveling under a clear blue sky full of sun. But that only went so far when you were so tired that just lying down and dying was starting to seem preferable to taking one… more… step.

Mira was about to surrender her pride and call out for Erik to stop when the big man topped one of the low hills and stopped on his own. Seska joined him as he stood looking out over the other side.

She dug deep into what remained of her reserves and trudged up the hill. Standing beside Erik on shaky legs, she looked down the other side and saw a wide, winding creek. Cottonwood, birch, and sycamore trees lined its flat banks.

"Is that…" She had to speak between breaths. "Are we… camping here… for the night?" *Say yes. Please, God, just say yes.*

"Yes," Erik replied.

"Thank you, God!" she cried and started down the hill, not even waiting for Erik or Seska. When she reached the creek bank, she let her knapsack slide from her shoulders and collapsed onto her back in the grass beneath a cluster of cottonwood and birch trees. She lay there with her eyes closed, taking deep breaths and feeling as though she could melt into the earth.

When she opened her eyes again, the sun had dropped down into the western sky. She must have fallen asleep. Or, just as likely, she simply passed out from exhaustion. She struggled to pull herself into a sitting position and felt every muscle in her body protest in pain.

She glanced around and saw Erik sitting on a log next to a small campfire. Seska was wading in the creek, occasionally pouncing and snapping at a startled fish.

She groaned and got to her feet. She stumbled over to her knapsack and dragged it to the campfire, sitting next to Erik on the log. He was whittling long sticks out of sycamore with the biggest knife she'd ever seen. It had to be at least twelve inches long and two inches wide. He already had a large pile of sticks, all about two feet long, and he appeared intent on doubling the size of the pile.

"What are those for?"

"Fish trap," he replied matter-of-factly.

She had no idea what he was talking about. She'd never heard of a "fish trap." She watched him whittle another couple of sticks before asking, "What's a fish trap?"

He finished the stick he was working on, set it on the pile, and picked up another sycamore branch.

"It traps fish."

Oh duh! Of course. A fish trap traps fish. That explains it all. How stupid of me.

She watched him work on the new stick for a while.

"I have a fishing line and hooks. We could just fish for the fish. You know, the old-fashioned way."

He continued working without replying. Mira decided she would wait until he was done so she could see how this "fish trap" thing worked.

About thirty minutes later, Erik slipped his gigantic knife back into its leather sheath on his belt, picked up an armload of the sharpened sticks, and waded out into the narrowest part of the creek. She watched as he placed the sticks close together in the creek, forming a tight V all the way across. He kept the downstream point of the V open. With another armload of sticks, he formed a tight circle at the narrow opening of the V.

Seeing the finished trap, Mira now understood how it was supposed to work, though she had her doubts about how successful it would be.

"Where did you learn to do that?" She asked when Erik returned to the fire.

"Someone showed me a long time ago."

"After the storm?"

"The day before."

That little bit of information astounded her. This was something Erik had learned on the very last day of the old world, back when he and billions of other people were absolutely sure they were going to wake up the next morning. But only a few of them did. It was knowledge that could have been lost forever but was carried on by a fifteen-year-old boy through a chance of fate. It was something real that bridged the gap between the old world and this one.

She looked back to the fish trap, memorizing its design, determined to remember how it was made so she could pass on the knowledge herself someday. Assuming it worked as its design implied.

"What did you do after the storm?" she asked. She didn't expect much of an answer, if any at all, but she decided she could keep trying. One of these days, she just might catch him off guard and he would slip up and tell her something personal about his past.

Just when she was beginning to think he would either remain silent or change the subject again, he replied.

"I went home."

She was so surprised she took a moment before seizing the opportunity to follow up with another question. "You weren't at home? Where were you?"

"A long way north, at a camp in the woods with some other kids."

She remembered how he'd described the storm and its aftermath.

"Did any of the other kids…?"

He shook his head.

"How long did it take you, to get home?"

He shrugged. "Two, three months. I don't remember."

"You went all that way by yourself? Did you meet anyone along the way?"

He sat for a moment before giving a slight nod. From her experience talking with him last night, she knew his hesitation was a sign he was about to clam up again. There was something there… Something had happened as he'd made his way back home, something he didn't want to talk about.

She backtracked.

"What did you do after you got home?"

"Came back north again."

She frowned. Either the end of the old world had been the most boring event in history, or he was leaving a whole lot of details out. She was pretty sure it was the latter.

"Why didn't you just keep going south, or go south later when the weather turned cold?"

Now he did clam up. He reached into his pocket and brought out a large hunk of venison jerky. Tearing off a bite, he stared out over the fire to the quickly approaching sunset, lost in thought again.

Mira sighed and dug into her knapsack for a smoked strip of goose. Getting to know Erik was like having a book in your hands with most of the pages glued shut.

Seska finally gave up trying to catch a fish and trotted back to Mira, lying down at her feet by the campfire. Mira gave her a piece of the smoked goose. After a while, she took out her father's map and spread it out on the log between herself and Erik, trying to locate where they were.

Estimating how far south and west they had traveled over the past three days, Mira drew her finger down the map to where she figured they were now. She guessed they were about two hundred or so miles due north of Nova Springs.

"If we head straight south now," she said, "it looks like we'll come out right on top of Nova Springs."

Erik glanced briefly at the map and then back to the setting sun. He took another bite of jerky, chewed on it slowly, and then stated flatly, "You can't go south."

For a moment, Mira was too stunned to say anything, not just by what he'd said but also by the way he said it, as if it was an undisputed fact.

"What do you mean?" she finally asked. "Why can't we go south?"

He swallowed the piece of jerky he'd been chewing, put the rest back into his pocket, and took a burning twig from the fire. Shaking the flame out, he reached over and used the burnt end of the twig to draw two dark lines of ash across her map. The lines were about an inch apart, the lower one being just north of Nova Springs.

"What's that?" she asked, a little annoyed about how he'd just messed up her map.

"The white."

"The what?"

"Ice and snow. A frozen wasteland. Nothing lives there. No one can cross it."

She frowned and looked at the map again. It sounded dubious at best. A region of ice and snow *south* of them? It didn't make sense.

"How do you know about it? Have you seen it?"

He nodded.

She thought about it and then said defiantly, "I've traveled through ice and snow before. We can get across."

Erik shook his head. "Nothing survives there. It's a death zone. It can't be crossed."

"How do you know that? Have you tried?"

He looked to the fire again and remained silent.

She thought back to when she'd first shown him the map in the cabin. He hadn't said anything about any frozen wasteland then. He knew she was going south and he'd even agreed they could travel together...

She got a sudden sinking feeling in the pit of her stomach.

"Where are we going?

He ignored her.

"Where are you taking me?" she demanded, more forcefully this time.

He cast a quick glance to her. She saw something akin to pity in his eyes. It infuriated her.

"Lakota village," he said. "You'll be safe there."

She had no idea what a Lakota village was but it didn't matter. Whatever it was, Erik must have been planning on dumping her off there from the beginning. That's why he'd agreed she could travel with him. He was leading her to this village where he could abandon her and then she'd be *their* problem. She felt a sense of utter betrayal.

"You think I'm helpless?" she asked angrily, her voice rising. "You think I need someone to take care of me? I was doing just fine before I met you." She stood and began walking away as fast as she could.

"I don't need you. I can get to Nova Springs on my own. I don't need anyone!"

Stalking up the bank of the creek, she wiped at her eyes, determined not to cry. Who in the hell did Erik think he was to just up and decide she needed looking after? She'd been doing fine on her own for almost a year now, ever since her father died. Her father taught her how to hunt and fish, how to set snares, where to find shelter, and how to start a fire. He'd taught her everything she needed to know in order to survive on her own. *He* had trusted her. *He* had believed in her. She sure as hell didn't need Erik or anyone else deciding she needed looking after. She didn't need any goddamn babysitter!

She walked for a long time with her head down, stewing in anger, until at last she came to a sharp bend in the creek where the bank was steep and cut away by the current. Sitting down on the edge, she stared into the water, watching small bits of ice float by and thinking about her father. She couldn't remember a time when he hadn't been teaching her something or giving her advice. He'd known someday he wouldn't be there, and he'd been determined she would have all the skills and knowledge she needed to survive on her own.

You can do anything you have a mind to, he'd often told her. *It might be difficult. It might take several tries. But if you stay focused and never give up, you can do it.*

She was going south to Nova Springs. That was *her* mind. If there really was some stretch of frozen wasteland down there barring her path, she would find a way around or through it. Erik couldn't stop her from trying. No one could.

She thought about Erik and his disapproving attitude when he'd first seen her under the collapsed overpass. So what? He didn't know her. He didn't know anything about her or what her father taught her. He'd never seen her hunt or fish or survive on her own. All he'd seen was a few minutes of her life when she was cornered by three men. He'd based his whole judgment of her on that one event. It wasn't fair and it wasn't right.

She took a mental pause and thought about that. Her father taught her never to get trapped without a second or third way out. *A cave is a grave,* he'd said. *You never know what's going to wander in and block your escape.* And hadn't that collapsed overpass been nothing more than a concrete cave?

If it was her father who had shown up instead of Erik, she could imagine he would have given her the same disapproving look and tone of voice she'd gotten from Erik, probably more so. And he would certainly have called into question her ability to make good survival decisions.

She considered what Erik knew about her – she was a young girl who, despite traveling with a wolf as a companion, managed to get herself cornered alone by three men who had just slaughtered a family. That was it. He knew nothing of what her father taught her, nothing of how she'd spent the last year surviving on her own. From his point of view, she was in bad need of someone to look after and protect her before she got herself into another desperate situation.

She stared into the water, conflicted between her anger at Erik and her understanding of why he thought he needed to take her to this village. "You'll be safe there," he'd said, and that pretty much summed it up. She had given him no reason to believe she could take care of herself. He was simply trying to make sure she was safe.

She glanced up from the creek. The sun was already setting. Its brilliant orange glow was quickly fading from the western sky. A crescent moon was rising in the east and stars were beginning to crowd the evening sky above her.

She looked back down along the creek but could not see the glow from Erik's campfire. How far had she walked? She didn't know. She'd been too angry and upset to pay attention. She stood and started back, feeling the chill of the night air already seeping into her clothes. Yeah, Erik was sure to believe she could take care of herself now. Foolish little girl throws a temper tantrum and goes storming off into the freezing night without so much as a coat. She didn't even have her knapsack with her. She had no food and nothing to start a fire with.

She wrapped her arms around herself and pressed on. She would go to this Lakota village. It was what Erik wanted. It's what he thought was best for her. But that didn't mean she had to stay there. Tomorrow, the next day, next week... she would start south again. No one could stop her from trying.

After about twenty minutes, Mira began to shiver. She picked up her pace, constantly glancing ahead, hoping to see the glow from the campfire. A crazy idea occurred to her that she might be walking in the wrong direction but she quickly dismissed it. She had walked upstream. She was sure of it. Now she was walking downstream. But had there been a fork in the creek? She couldn't remember.

After another ten minutes, she was beginning to feel a twinge of panic. How could she have walked so far in such a short amount of time? If she was caught out here all night without a coat or means to make a fire, she would be dead by morning.

Rescue and reassurance appeared out of the dark ahead in the form of a large gray wolf trotting towards her, wagging its tail. She gasped in relief and ran to Seska, catching the wolf in a tight hug around her neck.

"Oh my god," she cried in a laughing sob. "Don't you ever let me do anything that stupid again!"

Seska finished licking her face and then turned and started back down the creek with Mira by her side.

Erik was sitting on the same log and in the same position as when she'd left, leaning forward with his elbows on his knees, hands clasped together under his chin, gazing into the fire. The fire was built up much larger than it needed to be.

Mira guessed he'd done it so she could more easily find her way back in the dark, though she was sure he would never admit it. If he'd even glanced at her when she came into the firelight, she hadn't seen it.

She wondered. Did Erik send Seska to find her and bring her back, given the strange rapport she had witnessed between them? Or had Seska gone out after her on her own?

She sat down on another log next to the fire and let the warmth seep into her for a while.

"I'm sorry," she finally said. "You were just trying to do what you thought was best and I got all pissy with you." She glanced up at him. "I'll go to the village but that doesn't mean I'm going to stay there. I promised by father I would go south and that's what I'm going to do, no matter what."

Erik looked at her as if sizing up her resolve. He gave a single nod and turned his gaze back to the fire.

"You do what you have to do."

THIRTEEN

It was an old farmhouse surrounded by large, winter-bare trees and drifts of snow that came half-way up the first-story windows on all sides. Another two or three feet of snow lay on the roof and was drifted over the porch.

Inside was a spacious living room with a large couch, two chairs, and a low table in front of a fireplace full of cold ashes. On the couch lay a young girl wrapped in a thick blanket. She was pretty, with long, dark hair. Wrapped to her chin in a heavy blanket, she looked snug and warm. But her eyes were closed and they would never open again.

Oil had been poured all around the perimeter of the room and throughout all the other rooms, upstairs and down.

A boy entered the room from the hallway. He was tall, with broad shoulders, dark hair, and a lean face. He was wearing thick boots, a heavy coat, and carrying a backpack. He stood for a while, gazing into the cold fireplace, and then turned and carefully knelt by the couch. He lightly stroked the dead girl's cheek and hair.

"I'm sorry," he said quietly. "I thought I could take you to a better place. I tried."

He paused and closed his eyes before whispering, "I hope you find your way to a better life than this one."

He kissed her forehead and then stood. Turning, he strode to the door and out onto the snow-covered porch. He stopped and turned to take one last look at the girl on the couch. Then, holding the door open with one leg, he struck a match and tossed it into the house.

The fire raced quickly along the oil trail and throughout the house. The boy turned again, letting the door swing closed, and he walked out into the snow.

As the house became an inferno, the boy plodded through the deep snow to the nearby woods, never looking back.

Mira opened her eyes, feeling the sharp cold of the morning air on her face. She lay still for a while, staring up at the sky, the dream still fresh in her mind. Like her earlier dreams of the old woman in the frozen village, this one seemed real, as if she were there, watching everything happen in real life. But unlike the old woman, she'd felt as if she knew the boy, had known him for a long time.

Was he someone she was going to meet before the snow of the final winter began?

She wondered who the girl on the couch was. Would she meet her too?

The smell of roasting meat brought her out of her thoughts. She sat up and felt the warm, heavy weight of Erik's fur coat pressing down on her.

He must have covered her with it during the night or earlier that morning. She examined it more closely and saw it was made of bear hide with deep pockets. It was old and had been patched and repaired many times, but it was the warmest, most comfortable coat she'd ever felt.

She glanced to the campfire and saw a pheasant roasting slowly over glowing embers. Maybe that was the reason the rabbits and squirrels she cooked always had a slightly charred quality to them. She always roasted them directly over the flames.

Looking around, she saw no sign of Seska – probably out hunting – but Erik was standing in the creek with his back to her and his shirt off. He was washing himself with handfuls of sand and water.

Mira knew he was big and broad-shouldered, but the deerskins and heavy bear-hide coat he always wore belied just how muscular and fit he was. If he was fifteen when the storm brought the old world to an end, that would make him fifty-five now.

For an old guy, he was remarkably fit and in shape.

Erik rinsed himself off and then turned to start back up the bank to the campfire. As he did, Mira saw four wide, ragged scars raking down from his left shoulder and across his chest, even more horrendous than the scar across his neck. They must have been made by the bear that was his namesake. She'd never fully believed her father when he'd told her the bear got his name after killing a grizzly with just a knife. She'd thought it was a made-up story to explain his name.

She believed it now.

After forty years, it seemed unlikely this was his original coat. But that would mean he'd killed more grizzlies since then, and the only weapons she knew he carried were his staff and that big knife. She guessed her father was right when he'd told her the bear was the toughest sonofabitch in the woods.

As Erik stood by the fire putting his shirt on, Mira crawled out from under the heavy coat and dragged it over to the log next to him.

"Thank you for this," she said. "It was really warm."

He gave a simple nod and went back to closing his tunic with the leather ties along the sides.

Mira decided a bath sounded good and went to the edge of the creek. She glanced back to reassure herself Erik was busy with the pheasant before stripping down to her shorts and plunging fully into the water.

The creek was only a degree or two above freezing. She quickly resurfaced and let out a yelp.

Erik turned and watched her for a few seconds as she wrapped her arms around herself and bounced up and down in the water. Satisfied she wasn't drowning, he turned back to his pheasant.

Shivering but determined to tough it out, Mira knelt in the frigid water to her neck and hollered to Erik.

"Hey!"

He turned his head slightly.

"You didn't pee in this water, did you?"

He regarded her a moment and then turned back to the fire, shaking his head.

Mira grinned and began scooping up handfuls of sand from the bottom of the creek.

FOURTEEN

The pheasant meat, roasted over hot embers rather than direct flames, was tender and moist, more delicious than any Mira had ever roasted herself. It was just another reminder she could learn a lot about survival from this man. Not just basic survival, which she already had down, but how to make survival a little more enjoyable on a day-by-day basis.

As Mira helped herself to another piece of pheasant, Seska returned from her hunting trip and Erik went to check the fish trap he'd set up last night.

She watched as he reached into the water at the end of the trap and brought out a short rope holding seven large trout. He kicked open the end of the trap and left the rest of the sticks to be taken by the current before returning to the creek bank.

"Are you going to cook those or smoke them?" she asked as he stepped past her.

"Neither."

"So, you're just going to walk around all day with a bunch of fish over your shoulder?"

"Yep."

"Must be a mountain man thing," she whispered to Seska.

She glanced to the remains of the fish trap and then back to Erik.

"How did they get on the rope?"

He picked up his coat and staff before turning to her and giving a slight shrug.

"They do that sometimes."

"Do what?"

"You throw a rope in the water. They think it's a big worm and try to eat it. It gets caught in their gills. Fish are stupid."

Mira frowned. That didn't make any sense at all. In fact, it was probably the dumbest thing she had ever heard.

As Erik turned and started walking again, she caught just the hint of a grin beneath his thick beard.

"Oh God, you are such a *liar*!" she exclaimed, starting after him. "You put them on that rope before I woke up and then just left them in the water."

He neither admitted nor denied her accusation but his grin grew a little wider as he continued walking.

This was the first time she had seen any sort of a lighter side to the big man. He always seemed so morose and serious. She wondered what he'd been like as a boy.

Probably a troublemaker, she concluded.

As Erik and Seska knocked down the tall grass ahead of her, Mira glanced to the north and the dark line over the horizon. It was a little higher and wider again this morning, edging ever closer. She was positive now it was a harbinger of the final, great winter her father predicted and she'd been dreaming about. She felt it. At the rate it was approaching, she guessed it would be on top of them within a week.

Two hours later, they topped a long, low hill and were starting down the other side when Mira glanced ahead and stopped. She stared, feeling a sudden chill run down her back. For the first time since Erik mentioned the term, she understood that "Lakota" was the name of an Indian tribe.

The cluster of tipis was sitting across a shallow creek, right up next to the leading edge of a strip of woods. It was exactly as she had seen it in her dreams. The only things missing were the heavy, dark clouds and snow.

Both would be here within days.

She had never seen this village before, yet she had dreamed of it twice. The old woman had pointed to the bear, telling her to follow Erik, and he had led her here.

She wished she understood what it all meant.

Mira snapped herself out of her thoughts. Erik was about a hundred yards ahead of her now. Seska had stopped midway between them and turned to see what was keeping her. She started forward again and hurried to catch up with them.

Erik stopped at the edge of the creek and waited. When Mira finally joined him, he continued standing, looking at the village.

"What are we waiting for?" she asked.

He nodded ahead and she saw a tall, handsome man with long, reddish hair dressed in deerskins approaching them from the village. She felt another chill. He was one of the people she had seen frozen in the snow in her first dream.

The man stopped on the other side of the creek and waved for them to come across. Mira and Seska followed Erik across a line of broad, flat stones spanning a shallow part of the creek.

"Mato!" the man exclaimed, grasping one of Erik's hand and shaking it. "It's been a long time, my friend. I would say I'm surprised to see you but you would know better. She has been expecting you."

Erik nodded. "Good to see you, John."

"Tatanka will be here shortly. He'll take you up." The man glanced at Mira and smiled broadly. "And who is this pretty young lady?"

"Mira," she said in a much smaller voice than she intended. She felt herself blushing.

"Mira!" the man exclaimed, taking her hand in both of his. "That is a beautiful name. It suits you perfectly. My name is John. It's not very Indian sounding but what can you expect from a red bone?"

He let go of her hand and glanced at Seska, who was sitting on her haunches beside Mira, panting and watching everything with keen interest.

"And you travel with *sunkmanitu tanka*? You are truly favored by the spirits."

"Sunkmanitu what?" Mira asked.

"Sunkmanitu tanka. It means 'wolf' in our language. Lakota Sioux. We're all red bone here, part Lakota and part something else, except Tashina. She's full Lakota, probably the last of her kind."

As they'd been talking, another man approached them from the village. Mira guessed this man was Tatanka. He was a little shorter than John but large in body and with long, dark brown hair. He appeared much more serious as he approached John and said something Mira assumed was in their language. She didn't understand a word of it.

John listened, nodding, and then looked to Erik.

"Tashina would like to see you right away. I told you she was expecting you."

Erik handed the stringer of fish to John.

"For your people."

John accepted the fish and watched as Tatanka led Erik into the village. He then turned back to Mira.

"Tashina would like to speak with you too."

"Who's Tashina?"

"She is *wiyan wakan*, a holy woman. She is old and her wisdom is great. It is an honor to meet with her."

"But how does she know about me. We just got here."

He gave her an enigmatic smile. "There is very little Tashina does not know. She told us last week Mato would be visiting us soon and he would be accompanied by a young girl who walks with a wolf. We've been busy making arrangements."

He turned and indicated she should walk with him up into the village.

"Come, I'll show you around. Tonight, you can have dinner with my wife and me. Her name is Standing Willow. She's out gathering ingredients for a stew right now. She'll be excited to finally meet you."

Finally meet me? Mira wondered not only how she could have seen this place in her dreams, but also why. And how they could possibly have known last week that she, Erik, and Seska would be arriving together when she hadn't even met Erik until a few days ago.

She had a strong suspicion she'd probably seen this holy woman, Tashina, twice already.

As she and Seska walked with John into the village, Mira asked, "Why do you call Erik Mato?"

John laughed. "Mato means 'bear' in our language. It's a name he was known by many years ago. You've seen the scars?"

"The one on his neck or the ones on his chest?"

"His chest. He was attacked by a bear when he was a young man. He killed the bear with that big knife he carries in his belt. One thrust, right through the neck." He mimed jabbing a knife into the side of his own neck. "The story got around and he became known as the bear. He was quite the legend in these parts for a long time, though there are still some who think he's no more than a myth."

"You knew him when he was young?" she asked.

John shook his head. "I'm not that old. I first met him when I was about six or seven years old. He must have been in his thirties at the time. Our village used to trade with his. Some people still called him the bear but he was mostly tamed by then. A good woman will do that to even the roughest of men, and his was one of the best."

As they passed through the tipis, Mira noted a larger one sitting apart from the others. It had a big black bird painted on it. She didn't have to look inside to know there would be a fire surrounded by white stones in the center with an old woman seated on the other side.

Coming toward them was the shorter, older woman with the green blanket Mira remembered from her dream. The woman smiled at her and nodded but cast a nervous glance at Seska. Mira returned the smile and nod while trying not to think of snow alighting on the woman's bluish, frozen face. She walked with her hand touching the back of Seska's neck, keeping the wolf next to her and letting the people know they had nothing to fear.

She guessed there were fifteen or twenty people in the village, surely no more than that. They all appeared to be in their early thirties to late forties.

Apart from the dead woman and girl in the town by the river, she had never seen anyone under the age of thirty.

John stopped by another tipi and handed the stringer of fish to an older man and slightly younger woman sitting by a fire outside. He said something in Lakota before continuing with Mira's tour of the village.

"Erik was married?" she asked, going back to what John had said earlier. In all her conversations with Erik over the past few days, he'd never mentioned a wife. He'd talked about people he'd known, but never much about himself.

"He was," John said, nodding. "He even had a son. From what I hear, it was quite the love story. They met each other briefly when they were younger, right after the storm, but they got separated somehow. They both thought each other was dead for many years. She ended up leading a group of survivors trying to build a new life for themselves while he lived as a legendary bear-killing rogue in the woods. Then, by either chance or fate – Tashina would say fate – they found each other again. He came to her village to warn them about a band of heavily armed raiders heading their way. I guess it was quite the battle. A lot of people were killed. He damn near got himself killed in that fight."

"That's how he got the scar on his neck."

He nodded again. "I wasn't there, but from what I've heard, he went up against some big, bad-ass raider armed with an ax. It was a winner take all kind of thing. Erik just had that big staff he carries and his knife. He killed the raider but he almost got his head cut off in the fight. The leader of the raiders decided to go back on the winner-take-all deal after Erik killed his champion, and so Erik's wife walked right up to him and blew his head off with Erik's gun." He chuckled. "I told you she was one of the best. I don't know if my wife would do that for me."

They came to a fenced-in pasture where roughly a dozen horses nervously moved their grazing to the far end of the field, away from the wolf at Mira's side. John and Mira stood at the fence looking in.

"What happened?" Mira asked. "It sounds like he had a good life, a home. Why is he alone now?"

"The long winter. With summers getting shorter and winters longer, his community and some others they traded with got together and started moving south in small groups, but they started too late. The first groups started in the spring. That was the year winter arrived early and lasted for more than two years."

"That's when I was born," Mira said. "My father told me about it. He and my mother were in one of those groups. They got stopped before getting very far and took shelter in some houses along a river. He said a lot of people died. My own mother died only a few months after I was born."

"It was just bad luck. Everyone knew it was coming but no one thought it would happen so fast. Erik and his wife were in one of the lead groups, scouting ahead and preparing the way for the others. They got quite a ways south before the worst of the winter hit. But his son was in one of the later groups, bringing up the rear, and that was one of the many groups, like yours, that got stranded. Just being who he is, Erik went back, not even waiting for winter to end, looking for his son and anyone else who was stranded."

"Did he find him?"

John shook his head. "I don't think so. I know he searched for years, going back and forth over their trail many times. I guess after that much searching, he finally had to admit to himself they were likely dead. He stopped looking and tried going south again, but he was stopped by the southern ice."

"The southern ice?" She had a feeling she knew what he was going to tell her.

"Erik and some others call it the white. That's probably a better name for it anyway. It's a vast stretch of ice and snow, as far as you can see in any direction when you're in it. There's no way around and you can't go through it. The storms are deadly and there's no food, water, or shelter."

"Has anyone ever tried to cross it?"

"Erik did, trying to get back to his wife, and it damn near killed him. He had to turn back. And if the bear can't cross it, no one can. Others have gone into it but they've never come out again, not on this side anyway. And we've never heard of anyone from the south crossing it either, though I don't know why anyone would come north."

"So, he's trapped here," Mira said, mostly to herself. "He lost his son and he can't get back to his wife." Now she thought she understood why he was always staring at sunsets or into the fire.

"We are all trapped here," John said.

They both turned at the sound of Tatanka's approach. He spoke to John and then John turned to her.

"Tashina will speak with you now."

FIFTEEN

Tatanka led Mira and Seska to the tipi with the black bird painted on it and held the flap open. Seska darted inside before Mira could stop her.

It was exactly as she remembered from her dreams – the white rocks, the fire, the blankets – and sitting on the other side of the fire was the old woman with the colorful blanket around her shoulders. Though she had to be older than even Erik, she had the eyes of a much younger woman.

Seska trotted over and sat next to her. Tashina smiled and stroked the fur along her head and neck.

"So, you're the one who has brought us all together," she said, speaking to Seska. "You've come a long way, my friend. You have done well. But I'm afraid your journey isn't over yet."

Seska gave a low *woof* as if agreeing with her and then trotted back around the fire to Mira.

Tashina indicated the blanket next to the fire in front of Mira and smiled.

"Welcome, Mira. Please, sit."

Mira knelt on the blanket, her hands in her lap. Seska lay down beside her. She wanted to ask Tashina what she meant by Seska having brought them all together, and if she could really talk with animals. But she figured she was here to listen and not ask questions.

"Erik will take you south across the white," Tashina said.

Mira had expected the old woman to ask her some questions about herself, get to know her and then invite her to stay with them in the village. She was too stunned to say anything.

"My people will help you in any way we can," Tashina added. "They are already preparing food and supplies. You will leave tomorrow morning."

"No!" Mira finally said, surprising herself. "No, we can't. Erik said no one can cross the white. He's tried and failed. He said it's a death zone. Even John says it's impossible."

What was she doing? Just last night she'd gotten angry with Erik when he'd said she couldn't cross the white. She was even determined to go herself as soon as Erik left her in this village.

"Nothing is impossible if you set your mind to it," Tashina said.

Mira was taken aback, hearing the old woman speak her father's words.

"It will be difficult," Tashina continued. "But I see in you a strong will and an old spirit."

"No," Mira repeated, shaking her head. "It's too dangerous. I'll stay here, if not in this village than somewhere else. I don't want Erik or anyone else to risk their life for me."

"You cannot stay here. The great winter is coming. You know this. You have seen it to the north. You have seen it in your dreams. It will last for many generations. Nothing that is here now will survive."

"How do you know about my dreams?"

"Because I am in them," she replied as if the answer was obvious.

Mira had no idea how to reply to that so she took a breath and asked, "Then what's the difference? If we die here or in the white, what difference will it make?"

Tashina paused, as if thinking of how to put it in a way Mira would understand.

"I do not know if you will succeed or fail, but you must try. To stay here is to accept death. You would deny your path and the will of your spirit. There is a connection between the three of you, a connection that will be revealed in time. You did not meet Erik, any more than you found an orphaned wolf cub, by accident. The three of you have come together to complete a journey. You must go beyond the white. Mato will guide you. Sunkmanitu tanka will protect you. This is the path laid out long ago for the three of you."

How did this old woman know she'd found Seska as an orphaned cub?

"How do you know all of this?"

"Because I listen."

Mira almost growled in frustration.

"But what makes me so special, and why must Erik guide me? Why can't I just go on my own?"

"You are special, Mira, in ways you do not understand yet. One age of man is ending. A new age is beginning. Very few children have been born to this last generation. It is the way the land renews itself, sometimes with fire, sometimes with ice, but always with death and rebirth. You must survive. It is you and the others like you who will lead mankind into the new age. You are the bridge between the past and the future, the old world and the new."

Mira wasn't sure she understood, and she still wasn't ready to accept what the old woman seemed to believe was her destiny.

"What happens if I don't go? I could just stay north of the white and take my chances with everyone else in the great winter. Then what? Will the world end?"

"No," Tashina replied, smiling patiently. "There are other children. They are already south of the white. The Great Spirit has seen to it. You are the last. If you do not go, the world will continue. Mankind will still survive. But this is not your journey alone. Erik set out on his own journey many years ago to fulfill a promise, a promise that still haunts him. I believe this is why your paths have crossed and why the three of you have been saved for last. You must cross the white to safety. Erik and your wolf must be the ones to guide and protect you in order to complete all your paths."

Mira looked down at Seska, snoozing lightly beside her.

"What about Seska? You say she brought us together and that she must go with us. Why?"

"She is also an old spirit. She has chosen this path for reasons of her own. That is all I know."

Mira sat silently for a while, staring into the fire between them but not really seeing it. She felt like she was caught in the current of a river, being dragged downstream. She didn't like that feeling. If she went with the current, she had no idea where it would take her. But if she fought against it, she would surely drown. She had to work with it to get back to shore.

Finally, she let out a sigh. "Alright. I'll go. Not because I believe it's my destiny or because I have some great spiritual path to complete, but because I promised my father."

Tashina smiled and gave a single nod.

Mira stood and walked with Seska back to the opening of the tent. She paused and turned back to the old woman.

"You know the great winter is almost here. It is in the sky outside right now. What will happen to your people?"

"You have already seen it."

"But why don't you leave? You could go farther south, or west into the mountains, maybe find a new place to live."

"My people have lived on this land for generations beyond counting," Tashina said. "We are a part of it. While the great winter may take our bodies, it cannot take our spirits. When it is over and spring returns to this land, so will we."

SIXTEEN

Mira left the tipi with the black bird on it and wandered the village for a while with Seska beside her. Tatanka was not there when she left the tipi and she didn't know where either Erik or John were.

After a while, she found herself standing at the fence to the horse pasture again. She didn't even remember walking there. She glanced to the dark line of clouds to the north. She could see it over the tops of the trees now. She guessed it was less than a week away. Tashina had confirmed what she'd suspected. It was the leading edge of the final, great winter. It would be here soon. And then, as Tashina said, nothing here would survive. Of everything in her head defying understanding, that was the one thing she could grasp. That dark line was death. It was coming, getting closer every day, and there was no stopping it. The only chance she had of escaping it was to cross the white. And the only chance she had of reaching the other side alive was Erik.

She looked down at Seska sitting on her haunches beside her. The wolf looked up at her and gave a small whine.

"You and me both, girl," Mira said.

John found her a while later and brought her and Seska back to the tipi he shared with his wife. Standing Willow was, as her name implied, tall and slim, with long dark hair down to her waist. She looked exactly as Mira remembered from her dream, except this version of her was not frozen solid in the snow. She was warm and inviting, excited to meet both Mira and Seska, as John said she would be.

Mira asked them if they knew where Erik was.

John shrugged. "He doesn't stay around people for long. For him, two is a crowd. He's probably out in the woods again but I'm sure he'll be back by evening."

Several other men and women of the village gathered at John's tipi for a large dinner of stew, fresh and smoked wild game, mushrooms, various roots and nuts, wild berries, corn, squash, and other vegetables. Mira learned the village used to be located much farther north but had moved to follow the larger animals as they migrated farther and farther south. No one spoke of it but Mira knew they all understood what was coming and accepted it.

Even knowing their time was ending, these people would move no more.

When they were finished with the feast, the men gathered around a campfire while Standing Willow and some of the other women ushered Mira to another tipi. There, she was treated to a hot bath and a thorough scrubbing from head to toe. The women talked and laughed, excited to finally have a young girl to lavish their attentions on. Mira was embarrassed, feeling as though she was being treated like a living doll, but accepted all the attention with good nature and smiles. These women would never have another chance to pamper and preen someone her age ever again. The thought saddened her but she kept it to herself.

As two of the women brushed her hair and one trimmed her nails, three of the older women took Mira's measurements and quickly altered a set of deerskin clothing to her size. When Mira asked about the fate of her old clothes, the women laughed and pointed to the roaring campfire outside the tipi.

"Boys' clothes are for boys," Standing Willow explained. "And even a boy would not wear those rags."

It wasn't until early evening when Mira finally escaped with Seska and went to look for Erik along the western side of the village closest to the woods. John told her they kept a small, gray tent there for Erik's occasional visits.

She found the gray tent exactly where she'd seen it in her dream. Erik was sitting on a stump outside the tent next to a small campfire, rubbing rendered animal fat into the leather of his boots for waterproofing and conditioning. It was something Mira used to do with her own boots, but she had gotten out of the habit over the past year.

He glanced up briefly and then looked back to his boots, only to do a quick double-take and stare at her for what Mira felt was an uncomfortably long time. She had been thoroughly cleaned and dressed in the new deerskin clothing. Her long blonde hair had been washed and brushed out so it had a slight curl and her nails had been manicured.

"What?" she asked, feeling her face flush.

"You look…" He hesitated and then turned back to his boots. "You look like someone I used to know," he said quietly.

She took his reaction as the closest thing she would get to a compliment from him and sat down on the ground next to the fire. Seska lay down next to her. She stroked the wolf's fur for a few minutes before looking back up to Erik.

"Tashina says you've decided to take me south, across the white. I told her what you and John told me, that it's too dangerous, but she's insistent that we go."

When Erik didn't respond, she added, "We don't have to go if you don't want to. I'll stay here and you can go back to your woods." She had no intention of staying here but she didn't want Erik to know that. If he did, he would probably hang around the village indefinitely, dragging her butt back whenever she tried to head south.

Erik finished with the boot he was working on and stood. Before going into his tent for the night, he glanced down at Mira.

"You should get some sleep. We leave first thing in the morning."

SEVENTEEN

The entire village turned out to see them off, with the notable exception of Tashina.

As the men loaded packs of supplies onto the back of a horse and Erik talked with John, the women gathered around Mira and offered well-wishes and blessings in her language and theirs. The two women who had made Mira's new clothes now presented her with a coat similar to Erik's but made of layers of deer skin and rabbit fur. They added a hood, a pair of thick mittens, a scarf, and fur-lined boots. They knew where she and Erik were headed and must have worked all night to make sure she would be as warm as possible.

"Thank you," Mira said for what seemed like the hundredth time, returning their hugs and trying hard not to cry.

Standing Willow presented her with a necklace made of braided silver links. On the chain was a small feather made of finely carved bone.

"This was my mother's," Standing Willow said. "It has been passed down in my family from mother to daughter for five generations." She smiled but there was sadness in her eyes. "I know I will never have a daughter of my own, so I want you to have it. Please, pass it on to your own daughter when you have one and tell her our story." She slipped the chain over Mira's head and hugged her.

"I will," Mira whispered, no longer able to hold her tears back.

When Standing Willow let her go, Mira slipped the chain and pendant under her shirt next to the one her father had given her, feeling the weight of two legacies now entrusted to her and determined to fulfil both promises.

Erik declined the offer of a horse for himself so Mira also declined. She figured if Erik and Seska would both be walking, then so would she. She was saying her final goodbyes to Standing Willow and the other women of the village when she suddenly felt herself lifted off her feet and set down on the back of the pack horse.

"We'll move faster this way," Erik stated, as if his decision was final and unquestionable. He turned and took the horse's lead rope in one hand and his staff in the other.

Embarrassed and feeling like some princess that was being put on display, Mira squirmed around on the back of the horse, trying to find a way down, but Erik was already leading them away from the crowd of people.

"I wouldn't do that," John warned, walking beside the horse. "He'll tie you up there if he has to."

John stayed with them to the edge of the village. As they were crossing the creek, Mira turned and waved to him and the rest of the tribe. She finally saw Tashina standing before a campfire next to her tipi. The holy woman was chanting something in her language as she dipped handfuls of leafy branches into the fire before raising them into the air again several times.

Mira took one last, long look at the village, hoping to remember it as it was now and not as she'd seen it in her dreams. She was looking at not only the last of a proud people, but also the last of a world coming to an end.

EIGHTEEN

They made good time with Mira riding on the horse rather than struggling to keep up with Erik's long strides. By late afternoon, she guessed they had covered nearly three times the distance they would have if she'd been on foot.

They finally stopped for the day at a short stretch of woods. Mira had thought she was sore after following Erik across the prairie the first two days. But as Erik helped her off the horse and set her on the ground, she discovered a whole new world of pain. As soon as her weight was on her feet, her legs nearly buckled. Her butt felt like she'd been paddled with an iron bar.

"Oh God," she groaned, massaging her legs and rubbing her butt. "How do people ride these things? Couldn't they have given us a saddle or something? Maybe a pillow?"

Erik grinned and shook his head, looking amused by her suffering. He patted the horse's side and led it to the nearest tree.

Mira gingerly took a few small steps, stretching her muscles and feeling the blood starting to flow into her legs again. She walked out into the grass a little way while Erik tied the horse to the tree and unburdened it of their supply packs. Seska followed her out into the grass, running and bounding in circles around her as if showing off, panting and letting out a single bark every now and then.

"Where are you going?" Mira asked as she returned to where Erik had tied the horse. He was heading into the woods.

"To find dinner."

"Why can't we just eat what the Lakota gave us? We have plenty."

"We'll need everything we have for the white," Erik said over his shoulder. He disappeared into the trees.

By the time he returned, Mira had a campfire going and had set up the shelter the Lakota provided them. It was a larger version of Mira's own tent – a large canvas tarp that formed a kind of lean-to with covering for the ground. "This will work better in high winds," John had explained. "A regular tent would just get shredded or blown away and I don't think you want the trouble of putting up a tipi."

Mira hadn't asked what kind of winds could reduce a tent to shreds. She was sure she was going to find out for herself soon enough.

Erik walked into the small clearing of grass Seska had tromped flat and dropped a thick, seven-foot snake onto the ground by the campfire.

"What in the hell is that?" Mira asked, astonished by its size.

"Timber rattler."

"Those are poisonous."

"Only if they bite you."

She poked at it with a stick to assure herself it was dead.

"Where did you find it?"

"Sleeping under a log."

He sat down on one of the packs and drew out his huge knife. Mira watched as he cut the snake's head and rattle off, tossing them into the fire so Seska wouldn't be tempted to try and eat them. He peeled the skin off like a sock and tossed it into the fire, too, before proceeding to gut the snake. He let the organs fall to the ground. He must have felt it was okay for Seska to eat those. Finally, he wrapped the snake's body around a large stick and began roasting it over the fire, turning it slowly.

Seska sniffed at the snake organs and then turned and trotted out into the grass to hunt more palatable food for herself.

When the snake was done, Erik cut it into sections and showed Mira how to use her teeth to rake the meat off the ribs. Despite her misgivings about it being a poisonous serpent, she had to admit it was rather tasty. She'd never thought about eating snake before. It was another handy survival tip she would have to remember if they came out of this alive.

Seska returned as they were finishing the snake. She had nothing in her jaws but did have blood on her muzzle – evidence of a successful hunt.

With enough light still left in the day, Mira dug into her knapsack and brought her book out. She hadn't read it in several days. Seeing the book, Seska walked over and laid her head in Mira's lap, ready for her bedtime story.

"What is that?" Erik asked, eyeing the book.

"It's a story book. I found it in a house about a week ago. It's in perfect condition. I know it sounds silly but I like reading aloud to Seska. It's how my father taught me to read." She stroked the wolf's head. "I think she likes it."

Erik was still eying the book, a curious expression on his face, similar to the way he'd looked at her after the women in the Lakota village cleaned and dressed her up.

"It's *Alice's Adventures in Wonderland*," Mira said. "Have you read it?"

He nodded.

She turned back to the first page and began reading the story from the start. She had only been a few chapters into it anyway. As she read, she was aware of Erik listening while trying to appear otherwise.

She smiled to herself. Now she had an audience of two.

NINETEEN

They continued south through the rolling plains and small stretches of woods for several days, stopping only briefly in the afternoons for food and water, and then again in the evenings to hunt and camp. Mira's butt and legs finally grew accustomed to the back of the horse and the pain and stiffness gradually went away.

They quickly fell into a routine. Seska continued to hunt and occasionally brought back kills, but Erik and Mira provided most of their own food, always stopping for the day while there was still enough light in the sky for Erik to go hunting. Mira set her snares and would check them in the mornings, keeping her eyes out for mushrooms and wild fruits, berries, nuts, and vegetables. Twice they stopped along rivers where Mira tried her hand at fish traps and Erik fished the old-fashioned way. In addition to the fish, they were able to add a few river clams, frogs, and crayfish to their diet.

Every night before sunset, Mira took her book out and read aloud by the campfire. It was her favorite part of each day. Though he never admitted it, she suspected Erik also looked forward to it. He always came back from his evening hunting trips while there was still an hour's worth of light in the sky, whether he'd clubbed something to death with his big stick or not.

While they had managed to stay ahead of the dark weather front slowly creeping down from the north, it was still outpacing them and getting a little closer each day, taking up more and more of the northern sky. It had to be over the Lakota village by now.

While the temperature had briefly gotten warmer as they continued to move south, the past two days had been cold. An evening snow had fallen last night and this morning brought cold, misting rain that threatened to turn freezing.

By late afternoon, they came across an old ranch house and barn virtually hidden beneath the sprawling canopy of oak and ash trees. The house was leaning to the east and the barn's roof sagged dangerously in the middle, but both looked like they might continue standing for at least one more night. Because of the rain, Erik decided to make camp early. They stabled the horse in the barn and brought the supply packs into the ramshackle house with them.

While Mira started a fire in the old fireplace and Seska prowled the house for rodents and other possible treats, Erik picked up his staff and left the house, disappearing into the nearby woods.   As they had approached the house, he had stopped to investigate some animal tracks. Mira hadn't been able to see from the back of the horse what sort of animal had made them but she was sure whatever it was, it's what Erik had gone out to track and kill.

Once the fire was burning and warming the room as best it could with all the holes in the roof and missing windows, Mira joined Seska in prowling the house. Finding nothing of interest or use, she returned to the fire to wait for Erik. When he returned, they could eat dinner and Mira could read them another chapter from her book.

Warm in her new clothes and lulled by the crackling of the fire, she dozed off despite her efforts to stay awake.

She awoke to Seska's nose nuzzling her cheek. It was dark and the fire was down to a few sputtering flames. She glanced around. Erik wasn't back yet. She quickly got to her feet and went to the window. It was well past sunset. He should have been back more than two hours ago.

Seska went to the door, stared at it, and then glanced back to Mira, whining.

"Yeah," Mira agreed. "We'd better go find him."

She quickly built up the fire in the fireplace so it would give off more light through the windows and then fashioned a torch from a table leg and fabric from the old couch. Seska led her out into the night, sniffing the air and the ground.   The misting rain had finally stopped. Everything was coated with a fine layer of slick ice.

Mira hoped she would take a few steps into the darkness and then Erik would suddenly appear in her torchlight, giving her a what-the-hell-are-you-doing look. Maybe he had killed a deer and it was taking him a little longer tonight because he had to drag it back. That had to be it. He was just taking longer for some reason and she would meet him coming the other way. She wouldn't allow herself to think otherwise.

She followed Seska into the thick woods, hollering Erik's name. She wasn't sure if the wolf was really tracking him or not, but it made sense to her Erik would have come this way. She looked for signs – broken twigs, crushed leaves, scuffed rocks – before remembering she was trying to track a man who had spent most of his life in the woods and probably never left any sign at all.

She continued following Seska and hollering. She was beginning to worry how long the torch would last when they came upon a fully-grown bull moose lying dead in the leaves. It had no ice on it so it hadn't been dead long.

Mira cautiously approached the moose and looked it over. She could see where it had been clubbed on the side of the head. Its throat had been cut and there were knife marks around its left hind quarter. Erik must have ambushed it, probably stunning it with his staff first and then slicing its throat. The cut marks indicated he had begun to butcher it to bring the meat back in quarters.

But where was he now?

She searched around and found his knife lying in the leaves a few feet away. His staff was leaning against a nearby tree.

None of these were good signs.

"Where is he, Seska? Keep looking, girl. We've got to find him."

Seska circled the moose, sniffing at the ground, and then started off in a new direction. Mira followed. She could see a trail of freshly overturned leaves and broken twigs now. The trail zigzagged haphazardly through the woods, often going up against trees. On some of the leaves and on the trunk of one tree she saw small spatters of fresh blood.

Oh God. He's injured. He's injured and he's going the wrong way.

Seska suddenly ran and disappeared into the darkness ahead. Mira called out to her and hurried forward. A minute later, she heard the wolf barking just ahead of her and off to her right. What remained of her torchlight fell on Erik leaning with his shoulder against a tree. Seska was sitting on her haunches staring up at him.

Erik turned at the light. He was grimacing in pain and holding his left arm tight against his side. He was taking shallow, labored breaths.

Mira ran up to him. "Oh my god. What happened? Are you okay?"

He gave a feeble nod but Mira could see blood on his lips and beard.

"Damn moose," he wheezed. He coughed and blood sprayed from his mouth. He spat some more blood out and tried to take a deep breath, grimacing in pain again. "Thought it was dead. Went to cut it up and it kicked me. Think it broke a couple of ribs." He coughed again.

Mira was relieved that he was standing but she was still worried about him. Coughing up blood could mean a punctured lung.

"Come on," she said, putting her arm around his waist. "Can you walk? We've got to get you back to the house. You've been going the wrong way."

Erik glanced around, apparently surprised he of all people could lose his direction. "Shit," he muttered and pushed off the tree.

Mira couldn't support the man's weight but she could guide him. Her torch finally dead, she tossed it aside and stayed close behind Seska as the wolf led them out of the woods and back to the house.

Once in the house, Mira helped Erik to the old couch in front of the fire and eased his coat and shirt off. He had a massive purple bruise over the left side of his chest.

"Jesus," she breathed.

Erik gritted his teeth as she gently prodded his ribs with her fingertips.

After a few prods, Mira breathed a sigh of relief.

"I don't feel anything broken. But that's a pretty bad bruise and you're coughing up blood. You need to rest." She picked up his coat and used it as a blanket to cover him.

Erik leaned back and closed his eyes. "A good shot of whiskey is what I need." He gave a pained smile. "The whole bottle would be better. I don't suppose there's one laying around here anywhere, is there?"

"Not in this house. Seska and I already searched."

"You already searched for whiskey?"

"Stop talking and rest."

Finding a shallow pan in the kitchen of the house, she filled it with water, added a strip of venison jerky, and set it by the fire until it was hot. When it was done, she poured the broth into a tin cup and brought it to Erik.

"Here," she said. "Call it deer whiskey if you want. It's all we've got."

He downed the broth in one long gulp. Handing the cup back to Mira, he said, "Thanks, for coming out to find me. I must have gotten turned around out there after it kicked me."

"It was Seska who found you. She probably followed the smell of that coat."

He frowned and sniffed at his coat.

"You get some sleep," Mira said. "We may have to stay here a day or two until you're fit to travel again." She turned to refill the cup with broth but then turned back to him. "And no more hunting large game. You may be big, but you're too damn old to be tangling with anything much larger than a rabbit."

"What about the moose? It's still out there. That's a lot of meat. Can't let it go to waste."

"Don't worry about the damn moose," she said, refilling his cup. "I'll take care of it in the morning. I've cleaned large game before and I'm stronger than I look."

She brought the cup back and sat with him on the couch as he sipped at it, wondering how she was going to get several hundred pounds of moose meat back to the house.

After a while, she saw Erik had dozed off with the cup still in his hand. She took it, laid it on the floor, and then snuggled up against him under his coat, being careful not to touch his ribs. She'd grown fond of this big man with his gravelly voice and gruff ways. She didn't know what she would do if she suddenly lost him.

Feeling left out, Seska climbed onto the couch and curled up against Mira. Soon, all three were fast asleep.

TWENTY

Keeping Erik on the couch, Mira discovered, was like trying to train a wolf cub to sit while holding a raw steak in each hand.

"If you get up again," she said sternly, pushing him back down on the couch for the third time that day, "I'll have Seska take a chunk out of your arm. You can still walk with one arm." She turned to Seska, who was sitting on her haunches on the floor in front of Erik. "Seska, watch!" she commanded, pointing to Erik.

Seska looked from Erik to her and then back to Erik.

Erik studied the wolf cautiously, as if wondering whether it was worth the risk to find out if Mira was bluffing or not.

"You said you didn't train her," he said.

"I said I didn't train her to *hunt*."

Erik mulled it over before making himself comfortable on the couch, occasionally stealing glances to the wolf.

Satisfied he would stay on the couch now, Mira spent the entire rest of the day making trips into the woods and bringing back pieces of the moose as large as she could carry. She brought Erik's staff and knife back on her first trip. She left the staff in the house but decided his big knife was much more useful than her little dagger for cutting up a moose.

Each part of the moose she returned with – hind quarters, front quarters, back strap, loins – she quickly butchered and set to drying over the fire in the fireplace. The internal organs and trimmings, for the most part, she fed to Seska, who was soon too full to care if Erik got off the couch or not. Mira kept the heart and liver to cook for dinner that night.

"I can help with that," Erik had offered more than once.

"You can help by keeping your butt in that couch and healing," Mira retorted. "The faster you get better, the faster we can get out of here. And you're no good to anyone if you can't pull your own weight."

Erik was obviously unaccustomed to relying on someone else, and he made it known by grumbling under his breath every time Mira refused his help.

It took two entire days to finish her work on the moose, but by evening of the second day, Mira was satisfied with what she'd accomplished. She was exhausted, but she had managed to keep Erik on the couch almost the entire time and they now had enough moose meat, plus what the Lakota had given them, to last at least three or four weeks.

As exhausted as she was by the end of each day, she still found time to read one or two chapters from her book every night on the couch with Erik on one side of her and Seska on the other. Their full attention on her as she read made the hard work worthwhile.

The morning of the third day, Erik would no longer be kept on the couch. He insisted he could walk just fine and proved it by clumping around the house in his big boots. Mira could see he was trying like hell not to show any pain but he hadn't coughed any more blood since that first night, and even Seska seemed to be anxious to leave. Besides, she had looked outside that morning and saw the leading edge of the great winter was almost on top of them. If they waited any longer, they may well get trapped here by heavy snow.

They packed up the horse and started south again by midmorning.

"How much farther to the white?" Mira asked as Erik lifted her onto the horse, grimacing at the pain in his side.

"Two, maybe three days."

The snow started within hours of their leaving the house – big, heavy flakes that dropped straight down out of the sky. The snowfall steadily increased. By the time they made camp, it was coming down so heavy Mira couldn't see more than ten feet ahead of them.

The next morning, the dark clouds were directly over them and the heavy snow was still falling. It was now almost a foot deep. As they resumed their trek southwards, Mira turned to glance back to the north, as if she could see the Lakota village from here. The village had been experiencing this snow for at least a week now. She thought of Standing Willow, John, Tashina, the women who had made her clothing, and everyone else she had met there. They had known what was coming and had chosen to stay and accept their fate.

It will last for many generations, Tashina had said. Mira couldn't remember if the old woman told her that in person or in one of her dreams. It didn't matter. The great winter was finally here.

Nothing that is here now will survive.

Because of the snow, it took them a little over three days before they passed through a large stretch of woods and came out on the side of a hill overlooking an expansive, flat plain. Below them, at the foot of the long, steep hill, Mira could see the crumbling, snow-covered remains of a small town. But it was the plain beyond the town that filled her heart with dread.

"Is that... the white?" she asked, staring at a seemingly endless desert of ice and snow.

Erik nodded.

It wasn't just the endless, flat vastness of it that filled Mira with a sense of dread and hopelessness. It was the emptiness. There was nothing in the snowfield beyond, not even a single bush or tree stump. The woods below them and to the east and west stopped at the border of the white, forming a nearly straight line for as far as she could see in either direction. And in the sky above, the dark clouds of the great winter also stopped at the border, directly above where the trees stopped. It was as if there was some invisible barrier that nothing was allowed or even meant to cross.

"Abandon all hope, ye who enter here," Erik said quietly as he gazed out across the white.

It sounded familiar. Mira thought it must be a quote from a book but she couldn't quite place it. "Where is that from?" she asked.

Still staring out over the desolate expanse before them, he replied, "I've heard it's written on the gates of Hell."

TWENTY-ONE

Erik led them down the hill and into the town at the edge of the white. The buildings and houses here were in much better shape than any Mira had encountered before. She guessed it was because of the constant, frigid cold here along the border. They had not been rotted by sun and rain over the years as in every other town she'd been through. Though the town wasn't really in the white, it was close enough to where it was virtually frozen in time.

Erik chose the largest house in town, once probably the home of a rich person who considered the town and the surrounding lands his own personal kingdom. It was three stories of large, cut stone with intact windows and wide balconies on every floor. Erik unloaded the packs from the horse onto the front deck of the house and then removed the horse's halter and rope. He slapped it on its rump and sent it running back up the hill.

"We don't need it anymore?" Mira asked.

"We don't have any food or water for it," he said and nodded to the barren expanse beyond the town. "It would starve to death in there if the cold didn't kill it first."

Watching the horse run back up the hill and into the trees, Mira said, "It won't last long here either."

"Longer than where we're going."

"Why aren't there any trees in the white? They all just stop."

"The wind," he replied without elaborating. He began carrying the packs and supplies into the house.

Mira stared at the endless field of ice and snow and remembered what John had said about their simple canvas shelter, that it would hold up better than a tent against strong wind. She hadn't wanted to think about what that meant at the time but now she had no choice. They were about to challenge the white. John said it almost killed Erik once already, the man her father called the toughest sonofabitch in the woods.

What were they about to walk into?

Inside, the house was remarkably clean, as if the owners left only a few weeks ago. It was roomy, with marble floors, high ceilings, and elaborate wood trim. As they walked across the foyer, the emptiness of the house echoed with the sounds of their footsteps and the ticking of Seska's nails on the marble tiles.

They made their way to a large room with a fireplace, bookshelves, and several couches, chairs, and tables. The bookshelves were empty. What remained of the books were stacked in a few small piles by the fireplace alongside a large, jumbled pile of broken wood that looked to have been scavenged from the surrounding houses. It appeared someone had been living here not long ago. But the frozen-in-time nature of the place led Mira to believe that "not long ago" was probably more like ten or twenty years.

Erik tore pages from one of the books and started a fire in the fireplace while Seska prowled the perimeter of the room, sniffing everything. Mira examined some of the books in the pile. They all appeared to be about laws and taxes. She flipped through a few of the law books and wondered how on earth people of the old world ever got anything done with so many rules and laws. Who could remember them all? She found most of it incomprehensible anyway.

Erik fed several pieces of wood into the fire and then sat heavily onto the couch. He looked exhausted. Mira could see he was still in pain. He had been pushing himself hard this past couple of days.

"We'll stay here until tomorrow," she announced, though it was still early in the day. "You rest up. I'll take care of everything else."

"We need to clear the house," he said.

"What do you mean?"

"Make sure no one's living here."

"Too late for that. We've already started a fire. Besides, if anyone else was in here, I think they would have come to investigate by now."

"We still need to make sure." He started to push himself up from the couch. "Never know when there might be an old lady hiding in the pantry with a knife."

"Seska, watch!"

The wolf looked at her curiously and then at Erik.

"You sit and rest," Mira said. "I'll check the house."

Too exhausted to argue, Erik eased himself back down onto the couch. "Take Seska with you," he said. "Just in case."

"She can't keep an eye on you if she's with me, can she?" Mira said. "Don't worry about me. I'll be careful. And I'll even check the pantry." She quickly left the room before Erik could argue with her.

She wandered about the house, initially looking for the kitchen but then finding herself distracted by the faded artwork on the walls, the dusty marble busts of people long dead, the finely crafted furniture now warped and cracked with age, and the roomy bedrooms and bathrooms with all of their ancient finery.

She circled back to the living room and saw Erik had fallen asleep. Seska lay curled on the floor between him and the fireplace. She wondered if it was a common thing in the old world or something new, where women had to force men to take a break every now and again, just so they didn't work themselves to death trying to prove how tough and manly they were. She remembered the women in the Lakota village laughing about that very thing.

A wide, curving staircase with an intricately carved wooden railing and balusters led up to the second floor. Here, there were more bedrooms, closets and storage rooms, two more bathrooms, and another room behind two sliding wood doors. In this room was another fireplace, a desk and chairs, some small tables, and more bookshelves along the walls. Unlike the shelfs downstairs, these were still full of books.

Mira walked slowly along the shelfs, pulling out books and examining them. Now these were books she would love to read. There were volumes on history, art, music, science, medicine… a treasure-trove of knowledge from the old world and they were all in reasonable shape. She continued following the shelfs around the room, touching the spines of the books and wishing she had weeks or even months to stay here and read them – a wealth of knowledge on the verge of being lost forever.

When she reached the end of the shelfs along one wall, she turned back to the room to examine the other bookshelves and was startled to see a figure sitting in the chair in front of the cold fireplace.

She froze for a moment and then realized the figure wasn't moving, wasn't even alive. She hadn't seen it when she'd entered the room because the padded leather chair it was sitting in had a high back.

Even though the man was quite obviously dead, Mira approached cautiously. His skin was dry and leathery with a curious, yellow sheen to it. His eyes were dark, empty sockets. His lips had shrunken and pulled back, giving him a creepy, toothy smile. He was dressed in a fine, red silk robe with a scarf around his neck and slippers on his feet. Both the scarf and the robe had the letters STC embroidered on them.

She remembered Erik using the word "mummy" to describe how people looked after the storm. She had never seen one because all the mummies had eventually rotted away, leaving just their bones, hair, and clothing. But this was one of the mummies from the storm, she was sure of it. Why hadn't it rotted away like all the others? Had it been frozen in time like the rest of the house?

She leaned in close, examining its leathery skin. It almost looked wet. It had some kind of shiny coating on it that had turned yellow. She went to touch it with her finger when a voice suddenly spoke from the doorway.

"That's my father."

Mira jumped back and spun around, her heart racing.

A man was standing just inside the doorway to the room. He looked a little younger than Erik but not by much, with a thin build, long wispy red hair, and a scant beard. There were dark circles under his eyes, and his cheeks were sunken, making him look almost like a living mummy himself. He was dressed in an odd mix of both women's and men's clothing underneath an old military jacket.

"Don't let him scare you," the man said with a slight chuckle. "He's been dead a long time." He reached behind himself and eased the sliding doors closed.

Still speaking in a casual, friendly tone, he began to slowly approach her indirectly from across the room, letting his fingers trail along the tabletops and the backs of the chairs while he glanced here and there at the objects around him.

"This was his study. He spent hours in here reading his books and papers, smoking his pipe, sipping his whiskey. That was his favorite chair. He used to sit here every night reading in front of the fire. Even after everyone died, he stuck to his routine as though nothing at all was wrong with the world."

Mira backed slowly around the chair, keeping it between herself and the man as he continued to approach.

"My mother left when I was seven," the man said. "She walked out into a snowstorm one night and never came back." He stopped and placed his hand on the back of the chair, gazing upon the corpse of his father. "Dad died a few years later. I put him here because this was his favorite room. I used lacquer to try and preserve him but it didn't work very well."

He paused, continuing to stare almost wistfully at the corpse before looking back up to Mira. He frowned, as though seeing her for the first time.

"Who are you? What are you doing here? This is my father's room."

Mira didn't say anything. She glanced to the doors. Could she reach them, get them open, and get through them before the man caught her?

He started to move around the chair, a confused look on his face.

"Where's that big man you were with? And the dog. I saw you come into town together. You were riding a horse." He turned his head toward the door but his eyes stayed on Mira. "Where did you come from? Why are you here?"

Mira took her one chance and bolted for the doors.

Despite his age and frail appearance, the man had the reflexes of a cat. He almost caught her but Mira quickly turned and doubled back with the man just two steps behind her. As she darted around the chair, she pulled it over, tipping it and the corpse onto the floor as he reached for her. The man tried to leap over the chair but his foot caught and he tripped, falling forward, still reaching. His hand managed to grab the back of Mira's coat just before he hit the floor, pulling Mira back off her feet and onto the floor with him.

She screamed.

The man grabbed for her legs. Mira screamed again and kicked at him, her boots catching him in the face and shoulders. Unfazed, the man was like some crazy spider, scrambling forward and over her until he had her pinned to the floor.

Mira heard herself screaming for Seska and Erik while she flailed at him with her fists. The man was grinning now, panting, drooling as he tore at her coat and clothing. His nose was bleeding. His eyes were bulging with a frantic insanity.

Mira tore at his hair, and then a long-forgotten memory of something her father had once said came to her, something he'd told her when he'd been teaching her self-defense. She could hear his voice clearly.

It takes only four pounds of pressure to pop a man's eyeball.

She grabbed his head with both hands and savagely jammed her thumbs into his eyes. She used all her strength to try and push her thumbs all the way to the back of the man's skull. She felt his eyeballs pop. Even when blood and a clear, sticky fluid ran over her hands and arms and onto her face, she kept pushing.

The man let out a horrendous, high-pitched scream and rolled backwards off her, his hands going to his ruined eyes.

Mira quickly scrambled to her feet. The chair the man tripped over had broken. She grabbed one of the chair legs and turned back to him. He was wailing, crying, as he rolled back and forth on the floor, his hands still clasped over his face.

And then she was outside herself. She was watching some other girl bash the man's head over and over again with the broken chair leg. The other girl was crazed, insane with rage. She was screaming "God damn you!" with every swing of her club. Blood was flying everywhere, spattering the room and the girl's face, hair, and clothes. She kept swinging and screaming, even when the man's head was nothing more than a pulpy, bloody mess on the floor.

She felt arms reaching around her from behind and gently but firmly grasping her own arms, stopping her swings. Hands took the club from her and dropped it to the floor. She felt herself being turned away from the bloody remains of the man. The arms went around her again and pulled her close.

Mira slowly came back to herself. She felt the side of her face pressed against Erik's chest, his strong arms holding her tight. She was breathing heavily, panting. She tried to get ahold of herself, to calm down. And then all at once she burst into tears, bawling, crying like she had never cried before.

Erik continued to hold her, never saying a word. After a while she became aware of his hand stroking her hair and rubbing her back. She felt herself being picked up and carried out of the room and down the stairs.

He laid her on one of the big couches in front of the fire and placed his coat over her. Seska was there. Had she been with her and Erik up in the room? She must have been. The wolf licked her face and then climbed up onto the couch and lay next to her, placing her head upon Mira's chest and whining with concern.

Mira wrapped her arms around the wolf and hugged her, pushing the horror of the upstairs room from her mind and losing herself to the safe, warm comfort of Seska's thick fur.

TWENTY-TWO

She walked slowly through the living room, looking at the pictures on the shelves and table, at the books on the bookshelf, and the big leather couch that looked almost new. It was like the big farmhouse she'd seen earlier. All the windows were still intact. There were no holes in the roof and the house was free of dirt and debris. There was no smell of rot or decay. The floors didn't even creak or threaten to give way as she walked on them.

But the house was empty. It had the feel of having sat empty for a long while, as though whoever lived here left a long time ago and never came back.

There were three bedrooms down a short hallway. There was a master bedroom for the parents and a bedroom each for a boy and a girl. In the boy's bedroom, the bed was covered with sheets and blankets pulled tight and tucked in, with pillows arranged evenly along the headboard. In the other two, the beds were stripped of their sheets. In the parents' room, the blankets lay on the floor. In the other, the girl's, the blankets were on the bed and rumpled, as though someone had been sleeping there.

She moved to the kitchen and looked in the cupboards, the pantry, and the refrigerator. The cupboards and pantry held cans, packages, and boxes of food that still looked edible. None of the tin cans were bulging or rusty. None of the packages had moths or maggots in them. But the refrigerator was full of warm, spoiled food and discolored liquids.

On the kitchen counter was a white envelope with something written on it. She went to look at the envelope but movement outside the kitchen window caught her attention. Moving to the window, she looked out across a big wooden deck and a sunlit backyard to what she knew had once been a garden on the other side.

The boy was sitting on his knees in the garden. She knew him. He was the same boy she'd seen in the other house, the house he'd set fire to before walking into the woods. He was wearing a heavy jacket and a backpack. He was holding something flat and square in his hands. In front of him were three piles of dirt she recognized as graves.

He was crying. She was sad for him and wanted to tell him not to mourn for those he had lost. Everything would be okay.

Mira awoke on the couch with Erik kneeling in front of her, wiping her face and hair with a wet cloth. A pail of red-stained water was on the floor next to him.

She pushed herself up, feeling a little groggy. She didn't remember falling asleep but a quick glance at the windows told her she had been sleeping for hours. It was nearly dark outside. A fire was burning in the fireplace and Seska was lying on the floor in front of it, her head on her paws and her eyes watching Mira. Erik glanced up at her and then took her hands and began to wipe them clean.

Small bits of what happened upstairs began to come back to her. She could remember the books, a chair in front of the fireplace, and the corpse of a man sitting in the chair. There had been another man too, a skinny man with red hair. Where did he come from? He had smiled, talked to her, and then… her mind went blank. She looked at Erik wiping blood from her hands, at the pail of reddish water. She remembered Erik carrying her, laying her on the couch, and then Seska lying next to her.

"What happened?" she asked cautiously. She wasn't sure she wanted to know.

"You did what you had to do," Erik said. He finished wiping her hands and put the rag in the pail.

A brief image of a girl with blonde hair screaming hysterically, cursing, and swinging a club flashed through her mind. Mira closed her eyes, trying to force the image away. That girl was her. She had been crazed, violent, out of control. She had been so full of rage it terrified her. She began to tremble, afraid of the girl who had been hiding inside her all these years.

Erik sat on the couch next to her and put his arms around her, holding her until she stopped trembling.

"You did what you had to do," he repeated. "He would have killed you."

She felt herself relaxing in Erik's arms. The man had been insane. She knew he was trying to rape her and he was probably going to kill her when he was done. But instead of being terrified or trying to escape after disabling him, she'd suddenly been filled with a furious hatred toward him. She gouged his eyes out to stop his attack, but she hadn't killed him in self-defense or out of any fear for her own life.

She had beaten him to death because she wanted him dead.

That's what scared her – discovering she was capable of such murderous rage and violence.

Erik let her go and studied her face with a look of concern.

"I'm alright," she said, trying to reassure him with a smile. "It's just… I've never done anything like that before. I've never… been like that."

"Sometimes," he said, "you have to be like that."

TWENTY-THREE

Before they left the next morning, they scrounged through the house for anything small but useful. Mira found several more candles, some fishing line, and a larger sewing needle she figured might work better for repairing their heavy deerskins and canvas shelter. Erik found a good length of rope and enough material to build a kind of sled that would take the place of the horse in carrying their supplies across the snow. He also found a knapsack a little larger than the one Mira carried. He transferred some of their supplies to it and carried it over his own shoulders.

They found a small amount of rancid meat in the kitchen, along with a few loaves of rock-hard bread, rotten potatoes, moldy rice, and some rusted tin cans of food that were bulging and looked ready to burst. Some of the cans had been recently opened. Mira almost gagged when she thought about the man who had attacked her eating this. No wonder he had been skinny and out of his mind.

Mira and Seska joined Erik outside, where he had already loaded the sled and had the rope up around his shoulders. It was still snowing and the sky above was the heavy blue-black she was familiar with from her dreams. Just a quarter mile south though, beyond the boundary of the white, the sky was clear and the sun was shining. She had never seen anything like it and couldn't explain it. She doubted anyone could.

As they started forward, Erik stopped, glanced back to the house, and slapped his forehead with his palm.

"Oh shit. Did you remember to turn out the lights?"

"What?" Mira asked, glancing back to the house.

"Ah, to hell with it," he said, turning and starting forward again. "Let the next owners worry about the electric bill."

Mira hesitated, wondering what he was talking about. Lights? Electric bill? Why would he worry about those things? There had been no electricity for...

And then she realized she'd been had again, just like with the fish trap.

"Oh I get it. That's some *old*-world joke, isn't it? Something that only really *old* people would get. Well, you just keep crackin' 'em, old man. I'm sure someday we'll meet someone old enough to understand what the hell you're talking about."

Even though the boundary of the white was only a quarter mile away, it took them the better part of an hour to reach it because of the heavy snow. Once they crossed the boundary, Mira was astounded by the abrupt change. They went almost immediately from the dark, overcast sky and heavy snowfall to a clear, bright sky. The soft, heavy snow they had been trudging through became a hard-packed surface they would walk on as easily as bare ground. The only downside Mira could see was the sudden, extreme temperature drop. It went from freezing cold to painfully frigid in a matter of seconds.

"This isn't so bad," she said as they started into the white. "Except for the cold, it's easier walking here than back there."

"Don't let your guard down," Erik said. "When death comes here, it comes fast."

They pushed on through the day. When they finally stopped near evening, Mira glanced back and could still see the hills and trees in the distance. Out here though, distance was deceptive. She knew those hills and trees were several miles away.

"I don't get it," she said as Erik set up their shelter on the eastern side of a small hillock of packed snow. "Why do they just stop like that?" She was staring at the dark line of clouds that stopped at the boundary of the frozen wasteland.

"They're afraid," Erik said dryly.

"No, seriously. I've never seen anything like that before. Have you?"

Erik glanced at the line of clouds.

"I've seen a lot of strange things. Most times you can't explain them. You just learn to deal with them." He went back to working on their shelter.

Mira stared at the cloud line a while longer, thinking about it, and then decided Erik probably had the right attitude. It didn't matter what was causing the white or why the clouds of the great winter stopped at its boundary. They just had to accept it and keep pushing ahead.

Once the shelter was set up, Erik started a small fire for warmth, using some of the tinder the Lakota had packed for them. He set a tin cup full of snow next to the fire to melt for drinking water. Seska prowled the snowfield for a while looking for game before finally giving up and coming back to eat some dried moose meat.

When they were done eating, Mira took her book out and was able to read well into the evening. With the clear sky and the brilliant white snowfield all around them, the light of the moon and stars filled the entire area with a perpetual kind of twilight.

TWENTY-FOUR

She was beginning to think the white wasn't nearly as bad as Erik and John had led her to believe. After three days of travel, they were still under a clear sky. The air was frigid but the wind wasn't bad. She thought if it stayed like this, they would reach the other side with food and supplies to spare. Maybe the dangers of the white had mellowed or even disappeared over the years since Erik last tried to cross it.

The emptiness and isolation, though, were unnerving. They had long passed the point where she could see the hills and town from which they'd come. Now, all she could see was the flat, silent snowfield in every direction. She'd never thought of being able to feel the presence of life before, but out here in the white, she couldn't help but feel the absence of it.

Near the end of the third day, a west wind began to blow, quickly picking up strength. Fast-moving clouds soon rolled over the sky from west to east. The wind lifted a thin layer of loose snow and drove it across the frozen landscape with stinging force. Mira put her hood up and wrapped her scarf around her face. She could see Erik's beard beginning to ice up. Seska walked next to her with her head down.

"We need to stop," she hollered to Erik above the wind, her voice muffled by the scarf.

Erik hollered back, "Not here."

The wind continued to pick up strength. Soon, Mira could barely see Erik in front of her. This must have been the white's plan all along – lure the dumb humans in until they were too far to turn back and then kill them with a blizzard.

She could barely keep her eyes open against the stinging snow. She stumbled into Erik and thought he was finally stopping. Instead, she felt him tie a rope around her waist and then felt herself being tugged forward as he began moving again. How could he even tell what direction he was going?

She tried to keep her hand on the back of Seska's neck, worried the wolf might get lost in the whiteout. But Seska kept her head down and trudged unerringly forward as she followed Erik through the snow.

Sometime later – Mira had no idea how long, as the blizzard seemed to have obliterated all sense of time – she felt her foot catch on something and she stumbled and fell. Scrambling to get to her feet before the slack in Erik's rope ran out, she found herself staring into the empty eye sockets of a human skull. Some of the skin was still clinging to the bone but most of it had been scoured away by driving snow. Glancing around, she could also see a hand, part of a leg, and another skull with part of the spine and ribs jutting out of the snow a few feet away.

There were several bodies here.

She quickly got to her feet and hurried to catch up with Erik and Seska. Had those people also been lured into the white by a clear, calm sky? Did they stop and try to ride out a blizzard like this one, or had they doggedly trudged forward as Erik was doing now? How many more victims of this place lay buried in the snow under their feet?

When Erik finally stopped, it was at the bottom of a small hill Mira hadn't even realized they were walking on. The hill sheltered them from the wind a little but not much. Erik struggled with the canvas, the wind constantly trying to tear it from his hands. He finally had Mira sit on one end of it while he brought the other end up and over them to block the wind and snow. They didn't bother trying to stake it down. They just sat on one end and held the other over their heads and around their shoulders.

"Is this the wind you were talking about?" Mira shouted above the noise of the storm and the flapping canvas.

Erik shook his head. "This is just a blizzard. It's nothing."

This was *nothing*? Mira couldn't imagine what could be worse than this, what Erik thought was *something*.

Seska eagerly joined them under the canvas. Together, the three of them road the blizzard out until morning.

TWENTY-FIVE

"How do you even know what direction you're going?" Mira asked. They had started out that morning after digging themselves out of the snow and eating a quick breakfast of smoked fish and dried mushrooms the Lakota had supplied them with. She wondered if the fish was some of the trout Erik had caught with his fish trap.

It was now midday under a clear sky again and Mira realized she had no idea which way south was. Her unerring sense of direction must only work in the woods.

In answer to her question, Erik pointed directly ahead.

"Yeah, I know we're going that way," Mira said. "But is that south? How do you know which way south is?"

"South is south," he replied and pointed again. "That way."

Oh duh! she thought. *South is south. Of course. Must be something they teach you in mountain-man school.* She looked at Seska and whispered, "We're probably going in circles. Men never ask for directions."

By late afternoon, they were crossing a perfectly flat plain of ice and snow with Erik in the lead as usual when Mira heard a deep, muffled, booming sound coming from all around. She stopped and glanced around the snowfield, trying to locate the source. It sounded like distant thunder, but the sound was so low she could feel it in her bones.

A deep rumbling came from beneath her feet and the surface of the snow began dancing like drops of water on a hot skillet. A thin layer of fine snow rose into the air like a low mist. Seska was running back and forth, barking. Erik stopped and turned, also looking around.

Suddenly, the hard snowpack she'd been standing on became as fine as loose sand. Mira screamed as she felt herself quickly sinking past her knees into the snow. Just ahead of her, Seska let out a series of yips and a howl as her haunches sank deep and she struggled to stay on top of the once-solid surface.

Erik ran a few steps toward her and then he was sinking too. He fell forward onto the snow, spreading his weight out. He gripped one end his staff with both hands and pushed the other end out to her.

"Grab it," he shouted.

Mira grabbed for the end of the staff, missed, and then caught it on her second try. She pulled with all her might and felt herself slowly moving up and out of the snow as Erik pulled on the other end. Seska howled again and Mira saw the wolf was within reach. Letting go of the staff with one hand, she reached out and grabbed Seska by the scruff of her neck. She was still up to her waist in snow but Seska was almost under.

"Let her go," Erik hollered.

She ignored him and pulled with all her might with both arms. Seska was howling but Mira refused to let go. She kept a death-grip on the nape of Seska's neck, struggling to keep the wolf's head above the snow.

The rumbling stopped and the snow began to firm up almost immediately. Erik swung himself into a sitting position where he could get better leverage on the staff. Mira heard him yell something incoherent as he hauled back on the staff, dragging her free of the snow.

She let go of Erik's staff and turned to help Seska, digging with both hands. Seska gave one last, mighty heave and finally pulled herself free.

Mira crawled over to Erik and collapsed flat on her back beside him. Seska trotted around them, shook the snow from her fur, and then barked a couple of times. Finally deciding everything was alright, she sat down on her haunches next to Mira, panting and looking around as if nothing at all had just happened.

She took a couple of minutes to catch her breath. When she had felt herself sinking into the snow, she'd been terrified it wasn't going to stop and she was going to sink completely under until she was entombed. It all happened so fast. She had to replay it over in her mind to reassure herself she really was still alive and this wasn't some sort of last gasp of her imagination before she finally suffocated to death.

Rolling to her side, she looked at Erik. He was still sitting on the snow, catching his breath and looking out over the snowpack that had just tried to swallow them.

"What was that?" she asked. She had to ask a second time before Erik turned his head to look at her.

"I don't know. Earthquake, I think."

Mira knew what an earthquake was. She had felt a tremor once years ago and her father explained it to her. She knew what quicksand was too, which is what the snow had behaved like. But she'd never heard of one causing the other.

"Is it over?"

"For now," Erik said. "But if it was an earthquake, there may be others. Aftershocks. We'll have to be ready for them."

"You mean lie flat like you did?"

"Unless you can fly."

It took them nearly an hour to dig the sled out. One of the ropes holding the packs to the sled had broken and they lost two of the packs, almost one-third of their supplies. They continued digging for another hour before Erik declared it a lost cause and they started moving forward again.

Mira wondered how deep the snow beneath them was. She guessed maybe ten feet but was shocked a few minutes later when they came to a large crack that had opened up and was too wide to cross. Standing as close to the edge as she dared and looking into it, she saw it was more than fifty feet deep.

They zig-zagged across the snowfield, finding cracks narrow enough to cross with a long step or short jump. By evening they reached a wide valley with a flat bottom. Erik led them to the far edge of the valley before stopping to make camp.

"What if there's another earthquake?" Mira asked. "What if it happens while we're asleep?" She envisioned the shelter and everyone in it being sucked deep under the snow before they even had a chance to wake up.

"We should be safe here," Erik said. "This is a river. We're near the bank on the shallow side."

She was astounded. "What? A river? So, we'll just drown then?"

He shook his head. "The river is frozen solid under us and the snowpack is shallower here than anywhere else. This is the safest place."

As she helped him set up the shelter, she wondered what the white was going to throw at them next – a blizzard yesterday and an earthquake today. She dreaded what it was going to try to kill them with in the coming days.

They followed the river valley south for two days before leaving it when it turned to the east. They started out across the frozen plains again. While on the river, they felt two minor tremors – aftershocks, as Erik called them – but the ice and snow under them remained solid. Nevertheless, she noticed Erik now testing the snow ahead of them with his staff, feeling for hidden cracks beneath the surface.

The evening of the third day after leaving the riverbank, they witnessed the most breathtaking light show in the darkening sky Mira had ever seen. It was like the northern lights but on a colossal scale. Towering ribbons of red, green, and blue snaking across the sky above them, traveling with amazing speed from north to south. The colors were so bright and intense they reflected off the snowpack all around, filling their frozen world with breathtaking colors. Awestruck, Mira watched the lights for nearly an hour until they began to fade.

"Wow," she breathed, looking to Erik. "That was beautiful!"

He simply nodded.

She remembered what he'd told her about the storm, the event that ended the old world in a single night. He'd said it started with a bright flash of light to the west and then there were fast-moving waves of colored lights in the sky, like the lights they had just seen. The next morning, everyone was dead.

"It's going to be okay, isn't it?" she asked a little nervously. "There wasn't any flash this time. There wasn't any wind. It's not like the storm you saw, right?"

He put his arm around her shoulders and gave her a reassuring squeeze. "We'll be fine."

I hope, she added silently.

TWENTY-SIX

The next morning, they continued due south for several hours before Eric suddenly changed course to the southwest. Glancing ahead, Mira saw what had attracted Erik's attention.

"What's that?" she asked.

What looked like an enormous hunk of twisted metal was sticking out of the snow at an angle and towering at least twenty feet into the air.

"I don't know," he replied.

As they neared the object, Mira saw it was rising from the center of a deep crater in the snowpack. It was much larger and longer than she'd first thought, maybe forty feet long and fifteen feet wide. It was curved like half of a long cylinder, broken lengthwise and scorched black.

They stopped at the edge of the crater. Mira could see ice at the bottom, locking the object in.

Erik regarded it quietly for a while and then glanced around. Without saying anything, he directed Mira's gaze to several more craters in the distance. She could see smaller objects in some of them. They were also twisted and blackened.

"What are they?" she asked again.

He returned his gaze to the large object in the crater in front of them and nodded knowingly.

"Space station. Tyler and I talked about this. Looks like it finally came down."

"Space station?"

Erik explained how it was like a house but made of steel and orbiting high above the earth. People called astronauts would go up to it in rockets and live there for a while, performing experiments and studying things.

"After the storm," he said, "Tyler wondered how they would ever get back to Earth. We were camped under an overpass for the night and I told him to shut up and go to sleep."

Seska gave a single bark at the crashed station and Mira stroked her between the ears.

"Who was Tyler? Was he with you at that camp before the storm?"

He was staring at the wreckage, remembering or lost in thought. Finally, he said, "No. I met him about a week later and we traveled together for a while. He saved my life once." He paused before adding, "I couldn't save his."

She heard a little sadness and regret in his voice. Though she wanted to know more, she thought it best not to dig any deeper. She guessed this was an old wound for Erik and, unlike the scars on his body, it had never completely healed.

They stared at the silent monolith for a while longer before Erik turned and started south again. Mira and Seska fell in alongside him.

TWENTY-SEVEN

In the days following the lightshow in the sky and the crashed space station, they endured two more blizzards and three more whiteouts, each worse than the previous.

Mira was becoming worried. Not by the increasing frequency and violence of the windstorms, but because their supplies were running dangerously low. They were down to only what was in the packs on their backs now – maybe a few days' worth of rations, certainly not much more. Erik had abandoned the sled two days ago. She knew she had lost weight and Erik had too. Seska, though, really worried her. The wolf had lost a lot of weight. Mira could feel her ribs at night when she slept next to her.

"How much farther is it?" she had asked last night before reading from her book.

Erik had shaken his head and said tiredly, "A week, maybe. I don't know. It gets a little bigger every year. I don't know how far south it extends now."

"How long did it take you last time?"

"I didn't make it across last time. I didn't have enough supplies with me. I had to turn back after only a few days."

"So how do you know there's even another side? What if it just keeps going?"

"I crossed it a long time ago," he said, "during the long winter when I returned north. It wasn't this big or dangerous then." He thought for a moment and then added, "It's grown quite a bit since then, but it has to have a southern boundary. We just have to keep going until we find it. We've come too far to turn back."

She hoped he was right about the southern boundary. She knew he was right about having come too far to turn back.

She had lost count of the days they'd been in the white. She thought maybe it was two weeks but it could have been three or even longer. When they weren't hunkering down against a blizzard or another whiteout, they were silently trudging for hour upon hour, day after day, across the vast, frozen emptiness. Time had ceased to have any real meaning.

Half-way through a calm but not-particularly-sunny day, where the temperature was just above numbing, they topped a rise in the snow and found themselves looking out over what first appeared to be yet another seemingly endless stretch of snow and ice. It took Mira a moment to notice the odd, dark shapes clustered together in the distance. There were seven of them. They were large and square, rising out of the snow like half-buried monoliths.

She stared at them, unsure if they were real.

"Are those…? Is that… a city?"

Erik glanced up and studied the distant shapes for a moment.

"It was," he said before starting forward again.

Mira thought of the ruined city she and Seska had been through earlier – it seemed so long ago now. Those buildings had been hundreds of feet tall and surrounded by thousands of smaller buildings, houses, and other structures that spread out for miles. It was possible they were walking over part of the city right now, hidden deep beneath the frozen surface.

The buildings were a lot farther away than they appeared but Mira was used to the deceptive distances of the white. After several hours of trudging, they approached to within a half-mile of the first couple of buildings rising out of the ice.

Seska was trotting alongside Mira when she suddenly stopped and stood facing west. She let out a long, mournful howl.

Mira also stopped and looked, wondering what it was she was seeing. It was a bluish-gray wall, stretching across the horizon for as far as she could see to the north and south. It was moving toward them and rapidly growing in height.

She heard the distant roar of wind and a terrible feeling of dread arose inside her.

It was a massive snowstorm, much worse than any they'd encountered before – a roiling wall of ice and snow rising over a thousand feet in height and racing toward them at a frightening speed. It was still a couple of miles away but it would be on top of them within minutes.

Oh my god, she thought. All these days and weeks of struggle and survival had been for nothing. She remembered the bones she had stumbled over when they'd first entered the white – bones with the flesh scoured from them.

This was death coming. There was no escaping it.

Without a word, Erik grabbed her and threw her over his shoulder. She gripped onto his coat and hung on tight as he took off running as fast as he could toward the nearest of the buildings. His long strides carried them quickly over the hard snowpack but Mira feared it wouldn't be fast enough. The wall of snow was bearing down on them with incredible speed. Seska raced alongside them, the gray wolf flying across the snow.

Erik ran for the nearest building, its top two stories still above the snowpack. All of the windows were open, their glass long gone. Just beyond the building, the entire world had become a maelstrom of boiling snow and ice rushing toward them, mere seconds away.

Erik pulled Mira from his shoulder and shoved her through the nearest window. She tumbled and slid down a drift of snow all the way to the floor. Seska scrambled through the window and Erik followed.

"Get back as far as you can," Erik shouted, getting to his feet.

In the dusky light, Mira could just make out rows of desks and chairs. She hurried to the back of the room.

"Sit against the wall," Erik said. He took the roll of canvas for their shelter and wrapped it around and over them.

Seconds later, they were plunged into complete darkness as the storm slammed into the building. The deafening roar of the wind was louder than anything she'd ever heard. She could feel the walls and floor shudder. She felt snow swirling all around them, sneaking in under the canvas.

Mira put her head down and wrapped her arms around Seska. Erik wrapped his arms around both of them.

The storm seemed to last forever. The terrible roar of the wind was constant. She could feel the building thrumming under the onslaught. Several times, she both heard and felt a concussive bang as something heavy slammed into the outside of the building. She found herself worrying the building would collapse around them or the walls would be torn apart and they would be sucked out into the storm.

They huddled together under the canvas for nearly an hour before the worst of the storm was over. The wind continued to roar outside and a shudder would occasionally run through the building, but neither was as violent or terrifying as before. Nevertheless, Mira began to feel a sense of hopelessness welling up inside her. How could they fight something as big and deadly as the white? For all they knew, they might not even be halfway through it yet. They would be out of food in a few days and then they would starve to death. And even if they managed to survive another week or two, the next storm that rolled through would probably catch them in the open with no place to take shelter. Their little canvas tarp would be as useless as tissue paper against the storm that was howling outside right now.

They were going to die in this place.

"We're not going to make it, are we?"

For a moment she thought Erik had fallen asleep, but then his voice came out of the darkness next to her.

"Yes, you will."

"How? How do you know that? We're almost out of food and supplies and we don't even know how much farther we have to go."

There was a long pause before he answered again.

"Because I won't quit and I won't leave you behind."

He couldn't promise they would survive this or reach the other side. She knew that. No one could. But his promise he would never give up and not leave her behind reassured her. Though she'd known him only a few weeks, she felt if there was any chance of getting through the white alive, she was with the one man on Earth who could do it.

TWENTY-EIGHT

At some point during the night, Mira finally dozed off and fell asleep. When she awoke, it was still pitch black all around and eerily silent and still. The storm seemed to be over. Was it nighttime?

While she'd slept, she'd had another dream. In this one, she saw the same boy as in the previous two but he looked a little less haggard. He was standing next to a large pile of stones in a dry creek bed in the woods. The sky was all hazy, with just a few patches of blue visible. He laid his hands on the pile of stones and she saw the flat stone on top had words scratched on it. She could see the letters but they didn't spell anything she could read.

She heard the boy say, "We did have a good journey, didn't we?" And then he added, "I wish you could have been with me to the end." It was then she realized the pile of stones was a grave.

The boy turned and climbed up the steep bank to a concrete bridge. There, he'd stood a moment, staring down and looking incredibly sad. Finally, he'd said something else, touched two fingers to his head, and then turned and walked away.

She had been thinking about these dreams of the broad-shouldered boy the past few days – there wasn't much else to think about out here in the white – and she'd come to the conclusion they were dreams of the past. Not of her past but of Erik's. The boy not only resembled Erik, but many of the boy's mannerisms were similar to his. And the world the boy lived in was most certainly the old world, the world right after the storm when Erik was fifteen years old.

But how could she be dreaming of Erik's past? She didn't even understand how she could sometimes dream of her own future but she'd come to accept it. Her dreams of the future prepared her for what was coming. But what did these other dreams mean? How could seeing bits of Erik's life from forty years ago help her?

She wondered if the grave in the creek bed was for Tyler. Erik had said he couldn't save him.

She felt Seska still curled up next to her. They were still under the canvas but Erik was no longer under it with them. She heard a clicking sound and peeked out from under the canvas to see bright sparks flashing with each click several feet away. Erik was using his flint and steel to strike a fire.

Mira crawled out from under the canvas and felt fine, powdery, new snow under her hands. By the time she made her way through the clutter in the room to Erik, he had gotten a small fire going and was feeding pieces of wood into it.

"This is just for light," Erik said. "We need to keep it small or we'll fill the place with smoke."

She looked around and saw the giant snowdrift they had slid down. The window at the top was no longer visible. She guessed the building was completely buried now.

"How are we going to get out?" she asked.

He stood and looked up at the drift. "Dig."

"Can we eat something first?" she asked. "I'm starved and I'm sure Seska is too."

"We should conserve our supplies as much as we can," Erik said, "but I think I can help you out. Follow me." Taking a burning piece of wood from the fire, he led Mira and Seska out of the room and down a wide hallway to another, smaller room.

"What are these?" Mira asked, looking from one large metal box to another. Each had one side made of glass and inside each were rows of small, brightly colored packages.

"Vending machines." He kicked the front of one of the machines, shattering the glass. "Believe it or not, this is probably the only food from the old world that might still be safe to eat."

He reached inside and pulled out one of the bright packages. Tearing it open, he sniffed whatever was inside and then handed it to Mira.

"What is it?" she asked, also sniffing and then eying the contents warily.

"Potato chips. Those and the rest of this stuff aren't very nutritious but they have a lot of calories and salt, both of which we probably need. They should save us at least a day's worth of our own food."

Mira reached into the bag and pulled out one of the thin, oddly shaped things. She sniffed it again before taking a cautious nibble. Her eyes went wide at the crunchy, salty flavor and she quickly ate the rest of the chip.

"Oh my god! This is delicious!" She gave a few to Seska, who swallowed them without even chewing, before quickly finishing the rest of the chips herself.

"Don't eat too much too quickly," Erik said. "You'll get a stomachache and probably throw up."

He kicked through the glass of the other machines and began pulling more packages out, glancing briefly at them before putting some into his pack and tossing others aside.

Mira also began filling her pack, doing like Erik and tossing any of the packages that appeared swollen, torn, or just didn't look right. She ate something called a granola bar and gave Seska some popcorn and then some cheese sticks that were hard as wood but no match for the wolf's strong jaws. When she tried something called a chocolate bar, it was all she could do to keep from dropping her pack and eating every chocolate bar in the machine. Erik called it junk food, but she couldn't imagine anything tasting so wonderful being regarded as junk. After finishing the entire chocolate bar, she read the printing on the back of the package.

"What does it mean, BHA and BHT added to preserve freshness?"

"Better living through chemicals," he replied. "It's the only reason this stuff is still edible. That and the cold."

They filled their packs with as much of the unspoiled junk food as they could before returning to the room where Erik's fire was beginning to sputter. He added more wood, glanced around, and then broke a flat piece of steel off one of the desks not buried under snow. He used the piece of steel to help him climb the drift and then used it to begin digging.

Mira finished breaking the desk apart, securing her own piece of steel, and then climbed the drift to dig alongside Erik. Seska sat at the bottom of the drift, licking her chops and quietly watching them work.

"Was that the wind you and John were talking about?" Mira asked as she dug the steel into the snow and shoveled it away from where the window should be. "The reason nothing grows or survives here?"

"It comes through a few times a year," he replied. "I don't know how often but once is enough. If it catches you in the open, you can either say a quick prayer or bend over and kiss your ass goodbye. You won't have time to do both."

Now she understood why Erik thought the blizzards and whiteouts they'd previously experienced were "nothing," and why he hadn't wanted to try crossing the white again. If they had not been close to this city, if they hadn't reached this building in time... An image of the wind-scoured bones she'd seen in the whiteout weeks before came into her head again.

"Why did you decide to do this," Mira asked. "You said yourself the white is a death zone and impossible to cross."

"I had nothing better to do."

"Did Tashina talk you into it? Did she say something about me having a destiny or a path or something?"

"No."

"Then what did she say to you?" She was sure Tashina talked Erik into this somehow.

"She said, 'Don't take that girl with you. She'll just pester you with questions the whole way.'"

"Erik, I'm serious! I was going to wait until after you left the village and then try to reach Nova Springs by myself. If we're going to die in this place, I at least want to know why you decided to help me."

Erik paused in his shoveling and took a breath before looking at her. "Because I knew you were going to try and cross it by yourself. And I could either stay there and die with everyone else, or I could help you. Even if we don't make it, I'll have at least died trying."

"To get back to you wife?"

He stared at her, probably surprised she knew about his wife. Without saying anything, he turned back to the snow and began shoveling again.

"When we get across," she said, "I'll help you look for her. I don't have anything better to do, either."

TWENTY-NINE

They dug for several hours. Every now and then, one or the other would take a break to go down and add a little more wood to the fire. Even as small as it was, Mira noticed the air beginning to get a little smoky. They needed to either get out in the next hour or so, or they were going to have to douse the fire and dig in the dark.

They excavated a slanting shaft up through the snow from the window. Finally, after another fifteen or twenty feet, they broke through to the surface. It was daytime and Mira was briefly blinded by the sudden, bright sunlight.

She crawled out first, followed by Seska and then Erik. The building they'd been in was now completely hidden beneath at least ten feet of snow. Around them, buildings that had been visible before were now gone, while others that had been hidden under the snow were now partially exposed. Mira couldn't even guess how deep the snow had to be to hide an entire city.

As they traveled between the buildings, Mira became aware of an occasional, odd rumbling sound. At first, she thought it might be another earthquake or an aftershock, but then she dismissed the idea. This was different. It was more of a distinct sound coming from directly ahead of them. It was random. It would start out low, grow louder for a couple of seconds, and then just as quickly stop. The sounds grew louder with each building they passed and she could now feel the snowpack rumble beneath her feet.

At last, they came to where the snowfield began to slope down away from the city. There, they found the source of the rumblings. Mira stood beside Erik as he looked out over the chasm.

"Well, shit," he muttered.

It was a massive crack in the ground more than two hundred feet wide that ran from the northeast to the southwest, right through the southern edge of the buried city. The rumblings they had been hearing were buildings slowly toppling into the chasm and disappearing into the darkness below. Gigantic chunks of earth and massive blocks of snow and ice accompanied each building into the abyss.

"I think," Mira said, "we've found the source of the earthquake."

Looking across to the other side, she could now gauge the depth of the snow they were walking on. It was at least eighty or ninety feet deep, maybe even a hundred.

As she watched, another building on the opposite side of the chasm began to lean forward. The packed snow and ice around it began to break apart in huge chunks and fall into the darkness. The building continued to lean, picking up speed until it finally toppled forward with a great rumbling and crashing before disappearing forever.

Mira looked up and down the length of the chasm.

"How are we going to get across this?"

"We don't," Erik said. "We'll have to go around."

"This thing looks like it runs for at least ten miles in either direction."

"Yep," Erik sighed, "it certainly does." He turned and started walking southwest, parallel to the massive chasm.

Mira sighed too, and then she and Seska fell in behind him.

They followed the chasm for the next two days until it abruptly narrowed and then finally ended. Erik led them on for another mile or so after the chasm before turning south. When Mira asked why he did that, he explained the chasm might still stretch for a ways under the snow. He didn't want to be walking over a snow bridge only to have it suddenly collapse under them.

Good thinking, Mira thought. *Next time I have to cross a bottomless pit, I'll have to keep that in mind.*

Five days after leaving the city, their supplies ran out. The junk food from the vending machines had helped but not by much. Mira gave her last strip of jerky to Seska. Erik saw her do it but made no comment. They pushed on in silence, hungry, tired, and cold. When another whiteout hit, Mira simply wrapped her scarf around her face, cinched her hood down over her head, and trudged along with Seska at the end of Erik's rope. They no longer had the luxury of riding any but the worst of storms out.

Two days later, Mira was following Erik down a long, sloping hill of ice and snow when her legs failed her. She remembered falling and sliding a little way down the hill. She remembered thinking it was okay, that she would sleep now for a little while. She was just so tired.

When she opened her eyes, it was nighttime. She was looking up at the stars from the cradle of Erik's arms. He hadn't stopped. He had simply picked her up and continued walking. When she looked up at his face, all she saw was the grim determination of a man who would never stop, never give up until death finally took him.

She rolled in his arms to press her face to his chest. He held her closer and her arms went around the back of his neck.

She fell asleep again, feeling safer and more secure than she would remember for the rest of her days.

When she awoke again, she was in the shelter with Erik and Seska. Both were fast asleep. Next to her was a cup of water, melted from the inexhaustible supply of snow and kept from freezing by a handful of warm coals beneath the cup. Outside the tent, the sun was shining.

Had Erik carried her since yesterday and then all through the night. Had he carried her until his own strength was finally exhausted?

She sat up and left the tent, standing and looking around while drinking from the cup of water. She felt stronger today – hungry but stronger. The water helped.

All around her looked the same as it had for God knew how long. It was white – still the same endless expanse of ice and snow. She could barely discern the low, rolling hills around them because there was no other color. She had wondered before why Erik called it the white. Now, she could think of no other name for it.

Seska came out of the shelter, stretched, yawned, and then sat in the snow next to her. It broke Mira's heart to see how skinny the wolf was. If they didn't find food soon…

Erik stepped out of the shelter. He neither stretched nor yawned but stood and looked around for a moment or two as though he was some sort of ancient ice-king surveying the breadth of his domain. He then looked at Mira, sitting with her arm around Seska.

"How do you feel?"

"Better," she said. "I'm sorry. I just… I don't know what happened. Did you have to carry me all night?"

Erik glanced back out to the endless snowfield. "Don't worry about it. You're not that heavy." When he looked back to her, he asked, "Can you walk?"

Though she hadn't known him long, Mira had come to recognize when Erik was skirting a question or leaving critical information out. He had never lied to her that she knew of, but he could be creatively evasive. And he was being evasive now.

"How long was I out? How long did you have to carry me?"

His gaze returned to the white. After nearly a full minute, he finally said, "Two days."

"Jesus!" Mira exclaimed. "It this the first time you stopped to make camp?"

He said nothing for a moment or two. When he did finally answer, it was one of his non-answers that told her she had guessed the truth but he wasn't going to admit it.

"We need to keep moving while the weather is good. If you've got your strength back, we should get going."

Mira didn't push him to admit it but she kept her eye on him as she helped him take down and pack the shelter. He had carried her for two days before finally stopping to pitch camp and sleep for probably just a few hours. How in the hell was he still on his feet? And yet, as she watched him, she could see no sign of fatigue or anything else she could use in an argument to force him to accept more rest, not like she'd done at the cabin after he'd been kicked by the moose.

The man was inhuman... or superhuman.

With the shelter packed, Erik set out at an easy gait across the snow with his unerring sense of direction. Mira once again fell in behind him with Seska by her side.

THIRTY

It wasn't until they were following the floor of a wide, shallow valley when Mira came out of her trudging-daze long enough to notice trees rising out of the snow around them. They had already passed several. They were tree trunks mostly, with a few thick branches, but they were still standing and they were above the snow.

Despite her fatigue, which she was fighting with every ounce of her being, she felt a surge of hope the trees were a sign they were finally almost through. She cautioned herself, though. The white was not to be trusted. It was as ruthless as it was relentless. Maybe it left this spot relatively clear just so they would get their hopes up and let their guard down. Then, at last, it would kill them with one final storm or another earthquake. Maybe it would combine the two and throw in some lightning bolts or burning hail for laughs.

She had begun to think of the white not as a place, but as a cruel and insidious enemy.

The trees continued sporadically beyond the valley. For a while they disappeared entirely. But then they began to reappear in greater numbers. On the southern slopes of hills, Mira began to see occasional, small patches of bare ground. There was still not a speck of green anywhere, but the deep snowpack was finally giving way to lighter snow cover. She let herself begin to think that they were finally nearing the end of this frozen hell.

How long had it taken them to see trees and ground again? A month? Two? And how many miles had they traveled? She couldn't even guess.

They crossed over a deeper stretch of snow and then descended into another shallow valley. They were walking through a thin layer of loose snow and scattered stones when Seska suddenly turned, growled, and bolted past Mira, running back in the direction from which they had just come.

Mira turned and her heart nearly stopped.

Charging toward them on all fours was six hundred pounds of grizzly bear.

"Seska!" Mira screamed. The wolf was running toward the bear at full speed.

The bear stopped and rose up on its hind legs just as Seska attacked, snarling and biting at whatever part of the bear she could reach. The bear roared and swatted the wolf with one giant paw, sending Seska rolling through the snow. She immediately got to her feet and resumed her attack. The bear had dropped to all fours again and Seska was trying to go for its throat. The bear snapped its jaws at the wolf, just narrowly missing her spine.

Seska lunged again and latched onto the side of the bear's neck. She hung on as it reared up again, roaring angrily. The grizzly grabbed the wolf between its front paws and came slamming back to the ground. Seska yelped, letting go of the bear's neck. The bear grabbed her with its jaws and sent Seska flying with one mighty swing of its head. She landed in a cloud of snow and lay still.

The bear turned and began loping towards Mira, grunting and huffing with each bound.

Erik ran past her, charging the bear head-on. It turned to this new attacker and roared again. Erik swung his staff like a club, striking the bear alongside the head. He continued hitting the bear with such powerful blows they would have killed any other animal. He struck from one direction and then another, jumping back or to the side whenever the grizzly lunged or swung one of its massive paws.

The enraged bear suddenly lunged at him. Erik took one final swing with everything he had and broke his staff across the bear's skull with a loud crack. The bear swatted at him, this time connecting and knocking him to the ground. It swatted again, rolling Erik onto his back, and lunged at him.

Seska was suddenly in the fight again. She had gotten up and ran haltingly toward the bear. With its attention on Erik, Seska was able to grab onto one of the bear's ears. Snarling, she shook her head furiously, trying to rip the ear off.

The bear howled and reared up, trying to shake Seska loose. Erik quickly rolled over and got to his feet. He reached under his coat and drew out his knife. The bear came back down on all fours, right on top of Seska. Erik leapt onto its back. Holding on with one hand, he began furiously ramming the knife into the bear's neck.

The bear gave a roaring howl. It forgot about the wolf beneath it and swung its head back, its jaws snapping at Erik. He leaned back and held on with just his knees. Using both hands, he raised the knife into the air and brought it down with everything he had into the base of the bear's skull, driving it in all the way to the hilt.

In an instant, the bear collapsed and lay still. Erik also collapsed, rolling off the bear's back and onto the snow.

The entire fight had taken less than two minutes. At some point, Mira had dropped to her knees, clasping her hands to her mouth as she watched the horror unfold. For a long while, she continued to watch, breathless and horrified as neither Erik nor Seska moved. Finally, she got shakily to her feet and slowly approached. Great splatters of blood stained the snow all around. A huge pool of it was spreading out from under the grizzly's head.

Holding her breath, Mira approached closer and finally saw Erik move. Rolling over, he pushed himself to his knees and then laid his head back, uttering a loud groan and taking an enormous gasp of air. Mira, crying with relief, ran and threw her arms around him.

"Oh my god, are you alright?"

He took another deep breath and nodded wearily.

She glanced around and spotted Seska lying in the snow next to the bear. She wasn't moving.

"Oh no," she moaned. She cautiously approached the wolf, stopping a few feet from her. When she saw Seska's chest rise and fall, she ran the rest of the way and dropped to her knees next to her. She carefully lifted the wolf's head onto her lap and stroked her neck. Seska was bleeding from deep, ugly wounds all over her body but she was still alive.

Erik joined her and knelt next to her in the snow. He reached out and stroked the wolf's side.

Mira was crying. She knew Seska's injuries were mortal but she found herself asking anyway, "Is there anything we can do for her?" She looked up at Erik, pleading, hoping for some sort of miracle.

He closed his eyes and slowly shook his head.

Mira leaned forward and buried her face against Seska's neck, sobbing into her fur. She felt Erik's arm go around her shoulders.

She held her friend, her protector, her companion tightly against herself until long after Seska breathed her last.

When she was finally ready to let Seska go, Erik picked the wolf up and carried her down the valley to where the rocky bed of an old creek was relatively clear of snow. Erik lay the wolf down and began collecting stones, placing them around her body. Mira recognized what he was doing from her dream and soon joined him. Together, they built a stone cairn over Seska.

Mira sat staring at the cairn for a long time, remembering Seska first as a scared, half-starved cub caught in one of her snares, and then as her loyal companion and best friend, trotting along beside her wherever she went.

Every memory she had of Seska, even ones she had long forgotten, came back to her now. She treasured every one of them.

Erik found a flat rock and scratched something onto it with the tip of his knife. He laid it on the cairn, paused a moment, and then stepped back.

Mira could see the words on the stone. They were the same words she'd seen before in her dream.

"What does it say?" she asked.

"It's German," Erik said. "It means 'good journey, my friend.'"

THIRTY-ONE

Not long after they completed the cairn for Seska, Mira noticed fresh blood in the thin snow around them. It was all concentrated around Erik's footprints. Without a word, she walked up to him and pulled his coat open. The left side of his dear skin tunic had been completely shredded by the bear's claws and there were four deep, ragged gashes clear across his ribcage and stomach.

"Oh Jesus," she breathed. "We've got to get that sewn up right now. You're going to bleed to death."

For once, he did not argue. Mira sat him down and helped him strip down to his waist. The gashes were wide open and still oozing blood. They were right on top of the still-healing bruise from the moose kick but below his previous horrendous scars.

She was used to skinning and cleaning game but the raw ugliness of Erik's wounds was almost too much for her. Forcing herself to focus on the task at hand, she dug the needle and fishing line out of her knapsack and set to work stitching the wounds closed as best she could. The needle and line were far from sterile but Mira figured, without them, Erik would soon bleed to death anyway.

As she worked, she thought about the stone cairn in her dream and the one they had just made for Seska. Though she figured he wouldn't give her a straight answer, she decided to ask anyway. She wanted to know for sure if her dreams of Erik were real or not.

"Those stones you used to cover Seska... Have you ever built something like that before?"

"Many times," he said, hesitating only a moment.

"What about those words you wrote on that stone? Have you done that for all of them?"

He shook his head. "No, only the first time. For Tyler."

"In a creek with a bridge?"

He turned his head to look at her, frowning a little. She didn't think he would answer but then he turned his head forward again and said, "Yes."

"Why did you do it for Seska?"

"She earned it. She deserves it. Like Tyler did."

When Mira was done, she cut the lower half of his shirt into a long strip and used it as a binding over the stitches. She took a step back to assess her work and realized Erik had not flinched the entire time, hadn't even uttered a sound or changed his breathing. She wondered if he was so used to pain, he could ignore it when he chose to do so.

"You're going to have to take it easy for a while," she said. "I know we still have to keep moving, but if those stitches tear out, you're going to start bleeding again."

He regarded her curiously as she helped him put what remained of his shirt back on.

"Did you really teach Seska to watch?" he asked.

For a moment, Mira didn't know what he was talking about, and then she remembered.

"I never taught her anything. She always just seemed to know what I wanted or needed."

He glanced down, grinning, and shook his head. She had finally gotten him better than he'd ever gotten her.

Erik decided they would make camp in the creek bed. Mira helped him collect wood from the surrounding trees to build a fire, admonishing him whenever he tried to carry too much.

Once he had the fire going, Erik went back to retrieve his knife from the bear. It took him longer than Mira thought it should. Worried, she was about to go after him when he finally returned, his knife in his belt and one hind quarter of the bear on each shoulder.

"You're supposed to be taking it easy," she scolded him as he dropped the hindquarters by the campfire.

"This was easy."

Mira checked his bandage and stitches anyway. Luckily, they seemed okay.

"We can't eat those," she said, staring at the hindquarters and feeling her stomach churn. "That goddamn thing killed Seska. It almost killed you."

"All the more reason to eat it. Besides, we don't know how much farther we have to go before we find food." He drew his knife and began to skin one of the quarters. A moment later he stopped and glanced back to her.

"Seska gave her life to protect you. Don't let her sacrifice be in vain by letting yourself starve to death."

She knew he was right. They had run out of food days ago and they didn't know how much longer it would be before they found more. To let several hundred pounds of fresh meat go to waste while they were hungry would be the height of foolishness.

After skinning the quarters, Erik sliced the meat into strips and began drying them over the fire. When the first few strips were done, Mira forced herself to eat some. It was tough and had a gamey taste, probably because it had been killed in a fight. It felt bitter in her stomach but she forced herself to eat her fill, imagining the spirit of the bear looking down upon her from bear heaven and growling as it saw this tiny, weak human feasting on its flesh.

Fuck you, Mira thought back to the bear. *You killed my friend.*

After they had eaten, they finished drying the bear meat and packed it away. The had enough for several days even without rationing.

Mira pulled her book from her knapsack and sat down next to the pile of stones under which Seska lay. Erik came over and sat next to her.

Mira read the last two chapters, her voice halting and trailing off sometimes. When she was finished, she wiped her face, closed the book, and set it atop the cairn under the stone with the German words on it.

"Rest well, my friend," she whispered.

Erik put his arms around her and held her while she cried.

THIRTY-TWO

For the first night in a long time, Mira went to sleep not feeling hungry. Even so, she did not sleep well. She found herself waking up several times during the night, feeling cold and missing the warm, familiar comfort of Seska.

The next morning, while Erik packed up the shelter, Mira stood by Seska's cairn one last time, remembering all they had been through. A light snow had fallen during the night, dusting the rocks with a fine, white powder. After a while, she realized that Erik was standing behind her, fully packed and ready to go but waiting patiently.

"You will always be a part of me," she whispered. She wiped her eyes and then nodded to Erik that she was ready to go.

They left the creek bed and walked for hours under a cloudy sky in silence. For Mira, it didn't feel right not having Seska trotting along beside her. And though Erik never showed much in the way of emotion, she could tell the loss affected him too.

The next day was overcast again and it looked like more snow was on the way. Despite the cloudy sky and still-present snow cover, the weather had gradually been getting warmer over the last few days. It was still around freezing but it was no longer dangerous to walk without her mittens on or her hood up.

They were passing through more and more stands of trees now and occasional clumps of leafless bushes. There was still no green on them but they didn't appear completely dead like the first trees they'd seen. It was more like these trees were patiently waiting for spring.

As they went through a small cluster of trees, Erik snapped off a branch, looked at the broken end, and then handed it to Mira without comment. It wasn't dry and dead in the center. This was from a tree that could and probably would leaf out again if the weather warmed up. It had to mean they were out of the worst of the white now, maybe even out of it altogether and passing through the southern border.

She remembered the sharp boundary of the white to the north, the impossible way it formed a knife's-thin edge between two distinct climates. For whatever reason, the southern boundary wasn't like that at all. It seemed to be gradually tapering off, quietly fading into a warmer climate.

Erik picked up a long, almost straight tree branch and snapped the twigs off. It was thick and heavy.

Mira looked at him as he held it like a walking stick and shrugged.

"It's just not quite the same."

The staff he'd broken over the bear's head had been as much a part of him as the big, heavy, bear skin coat he wore. He probably felt naked without it.

He shook his head in agreement but kept the stick anyway.

They walked on for several hours. It was late in the day and snow had begun falling again when they came to another frozen river. As they were crossing it, Erik walked in the lead to test the ice. He had to outweigh Mira by more than a hundred pounds but it was Mira who fell through.

A loud crack echoed through the river valley. Mira froze, thinking it was the ice under Erik that was breaking. Instead, a large slab of ice beneath her own feet suddenly broke free and tilted out from under her, dumping her all at once into the river.

The frigid water felt like ten thousand needles all stabbing her at the same time. She struggled to the surface, gasping for breath but her lungs were paralyzed. She grabbed frantically at the edge of the slick ice but couldn't find anything to grip onto. As the current pulled her under, she was dimly aware of Erik running back to her.

And then the water closed over her head and she slipped into freezing darkness.

THIRTY-THREE

The two boys were laughing by the light of a campfire when the shorter, stockier one suddenly stopped and said, "Listen."

Erik listened. From somewhere far to the east came a long, mournful howl.

"Coyote?" he asked.

"Wolf," the other said. "Man, those things are so cool. Nobody fucks with a wolf. I remember when I was like six or seven years old and my folks took me to a zoo. When we came to the wolves, I stood there watching them for the longest time. My dad had to drag me away. I begged them for months to get me a wolf for a pet." He laughed. "I wanted the biggest, most badass animal in the woods for a pet, and what did they finally get me? A beagle."

"Could have been worse. They could have gotten you a toy poodle."

"Or a chihuahua," the boy agreed. "Man, I hate those barky little bastards. I think if I had to be reincarnated as any animal, it would be a wolf."

"What about a bear?" Erik asked. "I would think a grizzly bear could kick the shit out of a wolf."

"Only if it could catch it. But wolves are smarter. They hunt in packs. Ain't no grizzly going to fuck with a pack of wolves.

"Okay," Erik said. "You come back as a wolf and I'll be a bear. We'll have a smack-down and see who comes out on top."

"You're on!"

Mira opened her eyes. It took her a moment to focus and then she saw she was in the shelter. A large campfire was burning a few feet beyond the opening. She could feel the heat of it even in the tent. She saw her clothes spread out on sticks and branches all around the fire, drying. Erik was sitting beside her, staring out at the fire. She was lying under his heavy coat.

She coughed. Her chest hurt.

Erik turned at the sound of her coughing. He had the most worried look on his face Mira had ever seen. She tried to give him a reassuring smile but failed as another coughing fit came over her.

Erik stepped out of the shelter and quickly returned with a cup of hot broth. He helped her take a few sips. It tasted like that gamey old bear but it was warm and soothing.

"Thank you," Mira said in a hoarse whisper. Her throat was raw and scratchy.

Erik nodded and helped her take a couple more sips.

"How do you feel?"

"Tired. My chest hurts." She glanced back at her clothes drying around the fire. "Thank you for pulling me out. I don't know what happened. The ice just broke and then…" she stopped and began coughing again. Her lungs felt like they had froth in them, deep down inside where she couldn't quite cough it all out.

"Don't talk," Erik said, brushing her hair away from her face. "Get some rest. We're almost there."

She lay back down and was about to close her eyes when her dream came back to her.

I think if I had to be reincarnated as any animal, it would be a wolf.

"Your friend Tyler… You said he saved your life."

"He saved both our lives."

"But that's how he died, wasn't it? He died protecting you."

He nodded.

She smiled and closed her eyes. For the first time in a long while, she felt everything was going to be alright.

"Tashina said he chose this path," she said quietly before drifting off to sleep again.

She was playing with Seska in a rolling field of tall grass. It was summer. The air was warm and the sun was shining in a clear blue sky. Seska raced back and forth, bounding happily through the grass as Mira chased her. The wolf would stop and wait. Then, as Mira was about to grab her, she would dart away again. It was a game they had played many times when Seska was a puppy. Eventually, Seska would allow herself to be caught and then they would roll together in the grass for a while before Mira took off running with Seska chasing.

Seska stopped and waited. When Mira lunged, the wolf darted away, quick as lightning. Mira landed and rolled in the grass, coming up laughing.

Tashina was standing there, looking down at her and smiling.

Mira stood, glancing around for Seska but couldn't see her.

"Where did she go?"

"She is here," the old woman said, "waiting for you."

"I want to see her again."

"You will," Tashina said, "in time. But you need to go back now. Your journey is not yet complete. You still have so much to do."

"No, I want to stay here with Seska. Where is she?"

The old woman's patience was as infinite as her smile.

"You made a promise to Standing Willow, remember? You promised her that someday you would pass on her legacy to your own daughter."

Mira's hand went to her neck. Beneath her shirt, she felt the necklace with the fine bone feather Standing Willow had given to her. She pulled it out and looked at it, remembering her promise.

"And there is another promise you made."

Tashina held her closed hand out to Mira and then opened it.

When she opened her eyes again, Erik was no longer with her in the shelter. It was snowing a little now. She must have fallen asleep again. She saw her clothes were no longer hanging by the fire. Looking around, she saw them folded in a pile down by her feet with her necklaces and small knife and sheath on top.

She heard footsteps in the snow outside and then Erik appeared and ducked into the shelter. He sat down next to her. In his hand was another cup of steaming broth.

"You've been asleep quite a while," Erik said, handing her the cup. "How do you feel?"

"Better," she lied, accepting the cup and taking a sip. Her chest still hurt and she was struggling not to cough. She couldn't take a deep breath. Despite being under Erik's heavy coat, she felt chilled to her bones.

Erik placed his hand on her forehead and frowned. "You still have a fever."

"I'll be okay. Like you said, I just need some rest."

He watched her drink the rest of the broth and then took the cup and turned to her pile of clothes. When he turned back, he was holding her necklace. Not the one Standing Willow had given her, but the one her father had entrusted to her. He held it out in front of her, the small, deep blue pendant turning slowly, flashing in the light from the campfire.

"Where did you get this?"

Mira reached out and Erik placed it in her hand. She felt the weight of the little stone rabbit. It was heavy for its size. She had always liked it for that, as much as for its deep blue color.

"My father gave it to me before he died," she said, feeling the cool smoothness of the stone between her fingers. "He said it belonged to his mother and she gave it to him for luck. He wanted me to return it to her when I found her. That's why I was going to Nova Springs."

She looked up at Erik. He was staring at her with a strange, fixed expression, as if he was seeing her for the very first time.

"What was your father's name?"

"Chris. I think it was really Christopher but everyone called him Chris." She smiled, looking at the necklace again. "He said that this was my grandmother's most cherished thing. She called it 'magic bunny' but he didn't know why."

Erik stared at her a moment longer with that same strange expression, and then he suddenly stood and left the shelter, stepping out into the snow in two long strides.

She slipped the necklace over her head and then crawled out from under the heavy coat. She got dressed, slipping Standing Willow's necklace over her head too. She wanted to go out and ask Erik if everything was okay – he had seemed so strange, suddenly so lost and unsure of himself – but just the effort of putting her clothes on wore her out. She was still chilled but could feel sweat beading on her brow and running down her back. She lay back down and crawled under Erik's coat again.

She was just so tired.

THIRTY-FOUR

Mira awoke to cold darkness and snow stinging her face. She was moving, bouncing, but she wasn't walking or running.

It took her a moment to clear her head and focus her thoughts. It was night. She was being carried through a snowstorm. She had to be dreaming because Erik was running with her in his arms through a snowstorm at night.

"Stop," she tried to say but no sound came out. Her head was over Erik's shoulder and her arms were around his neck. When had he picked her up? How long had he been carrying her? She held on tight as he continued to run. This was no dream. What was he doing? She thought about his stitches. He was going to tear them loose and start bleeding again if he hadn't already.

"Stop!" she cried. This time she did hear her own voice. "Erik, stop!" She tried to turn her head to see where they were going but couldn't get turned around enough. "Erik, please! You'll rip your stitches!"

He either wasn't hearing her or he was ignoring her. He continued running, holding her tight in his arms. She realized he didn't have his pack on and she didn't have hers. He had left everything behind. What was he thinking? What was he doing?

"Erik, we have to stop," she cried. How long had he been running? Minutes? Hours? She cried for him to stop over and over until her voice began to tire and her cries became pleading, coughing sobs. He wouldn't stop. He kept running at the same pace through the snow and the darkness. All she could do was to hold on tight and keep pleading with him to stop until her voice finally gave out completely.

After another five or ten minutes, she felt his pace begin to slow. He stumbled, caught himself, and continued running for a few more minutes before stumbling again. This time he went down to his knees. He held her there for a few moments, tried to get back to his feet, and then fell forward onto the snow. Mira rolled out of his arms and then quickly scrambled back to him, grabbing his shoulder and trying to turn him over.

"Erik! Erik!"

His breaths were coming in deep, irregular gasps. Mira crawled over him so she could see his face and shook him.

"Erik, get up! We have to find shelter. We need to start a fire."

He opened his eyes. His gaze was random, unfocused at first, and then he looked at her.

"You're safe now," he whispered in his raspy voice. "You're safe. Look." His gaze shifted to something behind her.

Mira turned and looked in the direction Erik had been running. Three lights were approaching, bobbing in the darkness. It took her several seconds before she recognized them as torches. In the distance behind them was the light of a large campfire.

She turned back to him. "*We're* safe, Erik. *We're* safe now. We did it. We beat the white. We made it!"

He closed his eyes. "You're safe now..."

"No," she cried. She wrapped her arms around him as best she could, shaking him again. "Don't leave me. I don't want you to go."

His eyes fluttered open and he struggled to speak.

"I... have to." His voice was so weak she barely heard him.

He gave her a tired smile and closed his eyes one last time.

"You'll always be with me."

She cried and held him close, as tight as she could, her face pressed against his shoulder. She closed her own eyes, willing him to be okay with every bit of strength she had left.

The sound of horses came up from behind her. As if from a great distance, she heard men talking as they dismounted and approached.

"Holy shit, did they come from the north?"

"No way. No one lives in the north. It's completely frozen."

"They must have. Look at their tracks. Jesus, look at *them*! Look at how they're dressed."

"Oh my god... I think... I think that's the bear."

"The what?"

"The bear, goddammit. Don't you know anything? Look at him. I saw him once when I was like ten years old. That's the bear!"

"Whoever he is, he's bleeding like a sonofabitch."

"Who's the kid?"

"I don't know. Come on. Let's get them on the horses. We've got to get them to town, like right now."

THIRTY-FIVE

"I don't want you to go," she said, sniffling.

Erik got down on one knee in front of her. He was much younger now, not the grizzled, gruff old man who had found her in that cave, who had led her across the white, but a boy of fifteen. They were on the sidewalk outside his house in Iowa. Seska sat on her haunches next to Erik. Standing on the road behind him, waiting as patiently as ever, was Tashina.

"I don't want to go either," he said, "but you know I have to."

She was trying not to cry, to be brave for him, but it wasn't working. It was because of her he had to go away again.

"It's my fault."

He put his arms around her and pulled her close, hugging her so tight she wanted him to never let go.

"Hey, it's not your fault, not even a little. This began a long time ago, before even I can remember. But you know I will always come back for you. I will always find you, no matter what, no matter how long it takes."

For the first time in over a year, since she had lived with her father in the house by the river, Mira awoke in a bed. And for the first time in weeks, maybe a month or more, she was warm.

She looked around with just her eyes at first, reassuring herself this was not a dream. She was in a house. There was furniture around her – a dresser, a nightstand, a vanity with a mirror, a padded chair. Everything was clean and well-kept. There was glass in the windows and curtains over the glass. Filtered sunlight was streaming across the floor.

She turned her head and saw a woman sitting in a chair next to the bed. She was older, maybe a little older than Erik, and strikingly beautiful. She had long, dark hair streaked with gray and beautiful green eyes like her father's. Mira thought she looked as though she'd been crying. A tall, giant of a man with broad shoulders, blonde hair, and blue eyes was standing behind her, his hands on the woman's shoulders.

When the woman saw she was awake, she smiled and reached over, squeezing Mira's hand.

"Good morning, Mira," she said. "How do you feel?"

"Tired," Mira replied. She felt as if every bit of strength had been drained from her body. If the room were to suddenly catch fire, she doubted she would even be able to roll off the bed. Her chest still hurt a little but her breath came easier and she no longer felt chilled. She tried to ask the woman how she knew her name but the words came out all coarse and grating.

The big blonde man moved to her bedside. He was holding a cup of water with a straw in it. He placed the end of the straw between Mira's lips.

"Just a couple of sips at first," he cautioned. His gentle smile was the most comforting thing she had ever seen.

Mira sipped and felt the cool water work magic on her dry throat.

"That's enough for now," the man said, gently pulling the straw away. "Too much all at once will make you sick. You can have some more in a little bit."

"You've been here for several days," the woman said. "You were very sick. You've been awake a few times and told us your name, but you've been feverish and probably don't remember much. You had pneumonia. Thank God we still had some penicillin left. I think we've got you past the worst of it now."

"I... I remember the white," Mira said, her voice coming easier now. "The ice broke and I fell into the river. Erik saved me." She tried to look around. "Where is he? He was bleeding. Is he alright?"

The woman closed her eyes and squeezed Mira's hand tighter.

"You get some more rest," the blonde man said. Though he looked like a giant, he spoke in a soft, friendly voice. "My name is Eben, by the way. This is Ashley. If you need anything, just call for me. Okay? I will always be nearby."

The woman, Ashley, stood and Eben put his arm around her shoulders, leading her out of the room.

"Eben?" Mira called, as they were going out the door.

He stopped and turned. "Yes?"

"Where am I?"

He smiled. "You're in Nova Springs, my dear. Right where you're supposed to be."

She slept most of the next couple of days. Whenever she awoke, Ashley was there, sitting in the chair beside her bed. Eben was always there too, keeping her water cup full and bringing her small amounts of food – bread, crackers, small bites of meat, fruit, and a little cheese – increasing the amounts a little bit at a time as she regained her strength.

When she was finally able to stay awake for more than five or ten minutes at a stretch, Eben filled her in on what had happened after the three scouts found her and Erik at the edge of the white.

"They were hunting for a rogue grizzly bear," Eben said. "It was attacking our livestock pretty regularly for a couple of weeks. They tracked it to the edge of the white and were camped just outside the snowfield when they saw what they thought was the bear running toward them over the snow. They rode out to kill it but then realized it was a man carrying a child."

"Ironically," he continued with a smile, "it *was* the bear, just not the bear they were looking for. Erik must have seen their campfire in the distance and knew he had one chance to get you to safety. Our scouts said he ran with you in his arms for over three miles through that snowstorm."

"Erik and Seska killed the bear," Mira said. "It attacked us and they killed it."

"Seska? Is there someone else out there?"

Mira shook her head. "She's a wolf. I raised her from a puppy. The bear killed her. She was protecting me. We buried her under some stones in a creek."

"I'm so sorry," he said, gently. "Our scouts backtracked your trail and found your campsite and the remains of the bear. They said they found a small cairn but couldn't tell whose it was. If you want, we can have her body brought back here to be closer to you."

"No. Let her rest where she is." She had already mourned for Seska and didn't want anyone disturbing her body. If what Tashina said in her dream was true, Seska was waiting for her, and she would see her friend again in time.

She looked into Eben's eyes and then Ashley's and understood what it was they weren't telling her. She could still see Erik's tired smile as he lay in the snow, telling her she was safe. She asked what she already knew.

"Erik is dead, isn't he?"

Ashley's eyes brimmed with tears. She took Mira's hand and squeezed it. After a moment, she closed her eyes and nodded.

"Erik was the strongest man any of us will ever know," Eben said. "But his injuries were just too severe, and he used up the last of his strength bringing you to us. He saved you. You were so very sick. If he had waited even one more day, you would never have made it to this place."

Mira looked down at Ashley's hands holding hers. She was safe now, just as Erik promised.

Yes, you will, Erik answered when she'd asked if they would make it through the white. Only now did it occur to her that Erik said 'you' instead of 'we.' Had he always been prepared to sacrifice his life for hers?

She was sure he had.

She closed her eyes against the tears welling up in them. She had made it through the white and reached Nova Springs as she promised her father she would, as Tashina said she must, but it had cost so much – first Seska and now Erik. She loved them both, and they both had laid down their lives for hers. Mira's heart was suddenly filled with more sadness than she thought she could stand. Turning her face into her pillow, she cried for a long time before sleep finally took her again.

When she awoke, it was dark outside. Ashley was still sitting in the chair beside her bed, holding Mira's necklace in her hand, feeling the small, stone rabbit between her fingers. She had a sad, faraway look in her eyes.

"My father gave that to me before he died," Mira said. "He said it belonged to my grandmother. He wanted me to return it to her when I got to Nova Springs."

"Magic bunny," Ashley whispered softly. "Erik gave this to me a long time ago. It was his sister's and it meant a lot to him." She smiled. "It was his way of proposing to me."

She gazed at the little rabbit a few moments longer and then raised her eyes to Mira. "Erik was your grandfather."

Mira slid off the bed and Ashley got out of her chair, kneeling, holding her arms out. Mira came into them and they held each other for a long time.

THIRTY-SIX

Seven days after arriving in Nova Springs, Mira took a long, hot bath and dressed herself in the new, fresh clothing Ashley brought and slipped both her necklaces on, leaving them outside of her shirt this time. Ashley had given the silver chain with magic bunny on it back to her, telling Mira it was hers now.

She joined both Ashley and Eben in the living room of the house. She had spent the last two days of her recovery telling Ashley everything she could remember about her father, from how he kept their small group alive during the long winter to how he taught Mira everything he could to keep her safe when he knew he was dying and would no longer be around. Ashley listened quietly, crying often but sometimes laughing when something Mira said reminded her of a long-ago memory of her son.

Now, Ashley took her by one hand while Eben took the other. They walked with Mira between them out of the house and into the warm, late summer sun. The sky overhead was a clear, crystalline blue. To the west was a line of distant, snow-covered mountains. Far to the north, Mira could see the dark clouds that loomed over the white.

More than two hundred people stood along either side of the walkway and were gathered on the lush, green grass and under the trees all around. There were people of all ages – old men and old women, younger men and women in their twenties and thirties. Teenagers. There were even several children around Mira's age and younger. They all stood silently, respectfully, as Eben and Ashley led her down the long, stone walkway to the massive stone cairn at the end. Eben told her earlier every single person in Nova Springs had contributed to the cairn, each bringing their own stone in honor of Erik. Everyone in the village knew of his legend, just as every person in the village was his living legacy.

"If it wasn't for Erik and everything he did," Eben told her, "his strength, his courage, the sacrifices he made, none of us would be here today."

When they reached the cairn, one of the men who had gone back to retrieve Mira's knapsack and other items handed Eben the two halves of Erik's staff. Eben turned and handed them to Mira.

She stepped forward to the cairn and thought of Erik's final words to her – not what he said to her in the white, but what he said in her dream.

"You will always be with me," she said quietly.

She placed the two halves of the staff carefully upon the stones.

As she stepped back, Ashley laid her hands lightly on her shoulders. Mira reached up and took her hand.

"He kept his promise. He came back for me." She looked up at her grandmother. "I promised I would help him find you."

Ashley squeezed her hand and smiled.

"He did find me, through you. You brought him back to me."

With her other hand, Mira touched the little rabbit pendant on her necklace and looked back to the cairn.

I will find you again someday, no matter how long it takes. We will both find you. I promise.